The Pumpkin Code

Martin Smith

ISBN: 1987617118
ISBN-13: 978-1987617115

For Jean, Lindsay, Kirsty,
Christian and Anthony.

PART ONE

THE SECRET

1. WRONG PLACE

Years of backyard football had helped Artie Eason become an expert at getting a ball from a neighbour's garden.

He played football every day and, more often than not, he would have to pay a visit to a nearby property to retrieve a wild shot.

Or six.

But this was different.

He was hidden in a garden so far away that he could not even see his own house, which perhaps showed how bad Jack's final effort was.

It was supposed to have been the last shot of the evening before dinner.

Jack had taken his time with a long run up … and had smashed the ball way over Artie's head and the crossbar of the goal too.

The ball had flown out of sight into the deep, dark undergrowth at the far end of the garden.

Jack should have been the one to get the ball back. It had been his woeful shot, after all.

But it had not happened like that.

Instead Artie's friend had looked incredibly sheepish, made a quick apology with a small wave and slunk towards his house down the street without a backward glance.

That left Artie to retrieve his ball – as usual.

Artie had no worries about knocking on someone's door and politely asking for his ball back.

He had lived on the road all his life and knew almost everyone by name.

Most gave him it back without an issue. Others complained at the interruption but still let him collect his prized possession.

Some did not even bother to answer the door, which meant he had become rather skilled at getting in – and out – of nearby gardens undetected.

This though was more complicated.

This house was not on his street. He did not know who lived there. He could mostly match people's faces with their homes – even if the only contact between them was a waving hand from a car window – but not this time.

Jack's hoofed shot had somehow ended up in a garden in Bluebell Rose, the cul-de-sac of homes that backed on to his own road: Blenheim Road.

From the direction of his own garden, Artie knew exactly where the ball should be.

But, if he went and looked at the houses from the street, he would never know which door to knock on.

He had done the easy thing: he had vaulted his yard's wonky wooden panels and pushed through the dense bushes that separated the rows of gardens.

A quick climb of the tangled tree holding up a rickety old fence had got him back in sight of the ball again.

Satisfied that he could get the ball back easily, he dropped down from the tree and stood in the shadows.

Using the bushes as cover, he peeked at the garden in front of him. He had never been caught getting a ball back from a neighbour's garden – and he wasn't going to start now.

The ball was sitting in the middle of the home's back lawn. There was no other real cover apart from a shed on Artie's right-hand side.

It was quiet. Most of the kids would have disappeared for tea-time and people had yet to return from work.

Artie eyed the brightly lit kitchen with increasing dismay.

The window was even bigger than he first thought and the light radiating from the house cast an eerie glow over the lion's share of the lawn.

And part of the window was open too, meaning he could not afford to make any noise if he wished to remain undetected.

Artie stood motionless, watching the house for several minutes.

The lights were switched on both upstairs and downstairs but there did not appear to be any people moving around – in the section of the house he could see, at least.

His tummy grumbled. He was hungry.

Dinner would be on the table at any moment – his little brother Stanley would be tucking into chicken and pasta without a second thought about his older brother.

He needed that ball back.

He silently cursed Jack and his awful shooting skills – it should have been him here, sorting this mess out.

Artie shook his head.

Thoughts like that were pointless.

He needed to get ball back and get home.

Artie knew what he had to do: he could nip out of the shadows, grab it and be back to his own house inside two minutes. Easily.

He needed to get a move on – he was due to go trick or treating with Stanley and Fitch at 6.30pm.

A small voice inside his head reminded him: "It would have been done by now if you had gotten on with it."

Artie did not need any further encouragement. He leapt out of his hiding space.

The voice was always with him, acting like a guide when he needed it most.

It spoke to him occasionally, always pushing him a little bit further. Some people would have called him crazy but he never let it worry him.

He bounded over the grass in seconds.

His sporting instincts were strong: he kept low to the ground to snatch the ball on the run and save time.

He would be gone in a flash.

But a metre before his outstretched hands clasped around the leather football, Artie's foot sunk into an unseen hole.

He cried out in surprise as he fell, collapsing in a heap in the middle of the lawn.

His flailing arm had knocked the ball further away: It rolled slowly towards the house and came to a stop underneath the window.

Artie stumbled along on his hands and knees as he followed the ball's path. He reached the football underneath the window sill and tried to regain his breath.

The boy heard the danger before he saw it.

"What was that?" It was a deep, male voice coming from the direction of the kitchen. It did not sound friendly.

Artie's body went rigid with nerves. Moments later, he could hear a second voice too.

"What?"

"I thought I heard a thud outside."

"No, you're imagining it."

A shadow swept out of nowhere and spilled out on to the grass.

Artie watched as a second shadow emerged to join the first.

"See? I told you, Berry! Witless worrying when we have so much to do this evening!"

"OK, OK. I … just … thought I heard something."

The conversation stopped as they peered out into the garden. They scanned the empty lawn and the growing darkness beyond.

After several moments, the deeper voice spoke again.

"Look, we don't have time for this.

"It is Halloween. It is our big night of the year and we have a lot to do."

The worried voice replied with a snap.

"I know, I know. But if someone overheard our plans – even by accident – then it could ruin everything.

"We do not want to attract any unnecessary attention.

"Because, believe me, there will be plenty of that when they realise children are disappearing."

2. DECISIONS

The rough stonework grazed the side of his face as Artie pressed up against the kitchen wall.

He winced with pain but did not make a sound.

Something deep inside told him to remain hidden. There was a quiet menace in the voices above – a cold and calculating sound that made Artie want to run.

At the moment though, he could not.

He was trapped.

His legs were only a fraction away from falling into the light that beamed out from the kitchen window.

If he moved even a couple of centimetres, his shoes could be seen by the people above.

He said a silent prayer that the growth spurts his mother had long been predicting had not happened yet. For once, being short had its benefits.

Artie held his breath.

Part of him wanted to just stand up and take the consequences. True, he shouldn't have been there but would anyone really complain about an innocent kid trying to grab his football?

But instinct kept him still.

His heart was racing. What missing kids were they talking about?

He had not heard of anyone going missing in Foston recently.

Despite the fear in his stomach, Artie pushed himself a little higher up the wall so the top of his head rested against the bottom of the plastic window sill.

The voices were now muffled. It appeared the men had moved deeper into the house, away from the window.

Artie's right hand edged along the base of the wall.

Within seconds his fingertips nudged against the familiar leather of the trusty football.

He pulled the ball into his chest and prepared to make a quick getaway. His dinner was only a couple of minutes away.

But he had a new problem.

The bright light spilling out from the kitchen had knocked out his natural vision. Outside the patch of lawn that was bathed in bright light, he could barely see a thing past it.

His eyes sought out the mysterious hole that had so nearly landed him in big trouble. He had no idea what it was but he did not want to make the same mistake again on the way back.

Could the hole have been used for a washing line post perhaps?

Artie had no clue why it was there.

However, he had to make sure to avoid it this time. Otherwise he could be in serious trouble.

He shuddered.

Why did these people creep him out so much?

Everyone living in this neighbourhood were friendly, down-to-earth people.

These guys though seemed … wrong.

Artie couldn't describe it. He wanted to get a look at these men, who were talking about stealing kids. It could be important for the police.

He would snatch a look at them and be out of there as quick as a cheetah.

Slowly, he twisted his body so he faced the house. He left the ball on the ground and placed both hands on the window sill.

Centimetre by centimetre, the boy rose higher.

Finally, he could see into the house.

It was clean, freshly decorated and looked tidy. There was nothing out of the ordinary.

He ducked straight back down. Someone was sitting at the dining room table in the room to his left, concentrating intently on a set of papers.

Artie cursed.

It would only take the man to look up at the wrong time and he would be caught.

He dropped back down to his hiding place underneath the kitchen window and re-examined his options.

There was two ways to approach this, he thought to himself.

He could still get away.

As long as he stayed on his feet, he could be back in the trees and gone before anyone reached the window to spot him.

But something else made him stay put.

His heart was racing. Talk of disappearing children was wrong. These people – whoever they may be – were up to no good.

He could not leave it. He wasn't like that. He had to try to find out more.

Yet it was Halloween.

He was supposed to go out with Stanley and Fitch tonight. He had wasted enough time already. It was time to go.

Carefully Artie edged along the wall. His skinny jeans caught on the bricks, creating a tiny scraping sound, but it was not loud enough to attract further attention.

He peered around the corner of the house. Light spilled out of a back door on Artie's left.

A sturdy-looking wooden gate loomed large in front of him. The other side of the garden was hemmed in by the side wall of the detached garage.

Artie looked at the wooden beam running through the centre of the gate. It was the perfect foothold to vault the gate.

A single firm footing on that sturdy plank and he would be able to scramble up and over the gate in a flash.

It would take him a little longer to get home but the road seemed a safer option than a return to the darkness of the dense gardens.

Taking care to keep out of the light, he slithered like a crab back along the wall without a sound and scooped up his football with one arm.

Within seconds, he was back at the corner of the wall.

He was ready.

Slowly Artie eased around the corner, edged underneath a small window and towards the door.

He doubted anyone would be looking out of the back-door window pane but he did not want to take a chance of being seen when he was so close to getting away.

Yet the voice inside his head piped up again and made him hesitate.

"Why are children in danger?

"You need to help them. You can stop this happening."

Artie shook his head to try to clear his thoughts.

He answered out loud in a whisper: "No, I need to get home. Whatever this is, it doesn't feel right."

A shiver went down his spine. It was the first time he had admitted he was scared.

Artie Eason was known at school for being fearless. He was not the tallest, the biggest or the strongest in his year but he would never back down from a challenge.

Artie may have been the class practical joker but he was also as brave as a lion.

Yet this was different.

The voice inside his head piped up again. It was louder and more determined this time.

"You're right. Something isn't right here. But who else is going to help save those innocent children from these awful characters? No-one else knows, only you. This is all on you."

Artie paused. The voice was right.

He couldn't just run away from this and ignore it. It wouldn't be right.

With a deep breath, Artie tried to bring his racing heart under control.

There had to be another way into the house.

His eyes flashed up to the windows around the house. It was no good. Apart from the kitchen, they were all closed.

He tried to swallow even though his mouth was bone dry.

Dare he try the door?

"Do it." The voice was insistent.

Artie's hand snaked towards the white plastic door handle.

Five centimetres, three, one … his hand could feel the autumn chill running through the cold plastic door handle.

He froze and dropped the football. It bounced into a nearby bush.

Panic erupted inside his chest as a car door slammed close by.

Footsteps were coming in his direction – and they were getting louder.

With an awful squeak, the gate lock began to turn.

Someone else was coming into the back garden.

3. HIDDEN

Artie dived forward moments before the gate burst open.

He bit his tongue and ignored the pain as the heavy wooden door crashed into his arm.

He had moved not a moment too soon.

A short middle-aged woman with dark red hair waddled through the gateway towards the back door of the house.

Her arms were so full that she struggled to see the path ahead. A boot shot out behind her and kicked the gate closed without a backwards glance.

Again, Artie held his breath.

She was so close that he could have reached out and touched her if he wished.

He didn't though.

Instead, he pushed ever closer to the wood and hoped he would stay invisible.

Unaware that she was being watched, the woman chuntered to herself; the words were garbled so Artie could not understand.

But she did not sound happy as she stomped towards the light of the back door.

With a heave, the woman used one of her elbows to bang on the thick glass.

No-one came. The knock had been too faint for anyone inside to hear.

She did not bother again.

Instead she bellowed at the top of her voice. "For goodness sake, can someone open the blooming door!"

The woman, who looked to Artie like a witch with a curved nose and big eyes, sounded at the end of the tether.

Much to her annoyance, still no-one came to help her.

Taking care to make sure she did not drop anything; the woman juggled the objects in her arms to free up a hand.

Once she was set, she pushed down on the white handle and leaned into the door with her body weight.

The door handle responded and opened with a flourish.

The sudden movement caught the woman off-balance but she regained her footing at once and strode into the house without bothering to close the door behind her.

The opening meant Artie could now see into the house. It was a small utility room leading to a medium-sized kitchen.

The woman had walked straight through both rooms and out of sight.

The boy looked wistfully at the gateway.

He could now escape with ease. It was so tempting.

The football, of course, would be lost but at least

he would be away from this bunch of freaks.

Rubbing his throbbing arm, he edged out from his hiding place behind the gate.

The gateway stood directly in front of him and the door to the house was on his left.

Artie was caught in two minds.

Again, the voice spoke to him.

It did not mess about.

"You can't leave. They are bad people, you know that. You need to find out what they're up to."

He shook his head to try to stop the words coming. It did not work. Instead the voice got louder.

"Go inside. Something is clearly not right here – and you may be the only chance to stop them."

He could hear voices coming from the house.

The woman was speaking loudly: "OK. Let me put these down and close the door!

"I'll be with you in a moment!"

Artie had to make his mind up or he would be discovered.

His mind raced over the options.

He could escape out of the gate and flee back home without another thought about this strange encounter.

He could return to the back garden, grab his football, dodge the kitchen lights and make his way home through the undergrowth.

Or he could go into the house to try to find out what these rascals were up to.

The voice inside his head spoke again.

"There is only one choice. You know it."

Artie swallowed. He was unsure if he had the courage to do it. He could feel the sweat on his palms.

Looking down, he noticed his hands had curled into fists.

With gritted teeth, he reminded himself: "I'm Artie Eason and I'm not afraid of anything."

His mind was made up.

With a couple of long strides, he ducked into the house – and ignored the unusual feeling of fear that growled in the pit of his stomach.

Pinned between the freshly painted wall and the washing machine, Artie curled up under a counter in the utility room and tried to make himself as small as possible.

One close look in his direction and he would be discovered.

But there were dark shadows beneath the counter, which gave him some cover from prying eyes.

He made it just in time. Moments later, the woman stepped back into the room and closed the door.

Artie watched her push the door handle upwards to engage the lock and turn a key to trigger the mechanism.

She stopped and glanced behind her. It was almost as if she knew she was being watched.

Artie closed his eyes.

He waited.

She did not move.

"Gillian! I am waiting!"

The voice came from the kitchen. It was deep and gruff, like a large dog that had spotted intruders on its territory.

The woman opened a door directly in front of Artie, which revealed a small toilet and washbasin.

After she confirmed it was empty, she shrugged and returned to the kitchen.

She snapped: "I'm coming! For heaven's sake, give me a break!

"You lot sit around and expect me to do all the work. And then you have the cheek to complain about it too!"

Her voice trailed off as she moved deeper into the house. Again, she moved quicker than he expected for her age.

A door closed and the voices became muffled.

Finally, the boy released the stale air in his lungs and gulped down mouthfuls of fresh oxygen.

He could feel the sweat on his back as he began to wriggle out his hiding place. It had been close.

Artie's mind was racing.

The back door was now locked.

Even worse, the key was no longer wedged into the keyhole – that dratted woman must have taken it with her.

Artie frowned. His escape route had disappeared within a matter of seconds.

He edged out from the washing machine and crawled, crab-like, into the toilet.

It was tiny, barely enough room even for a skinny 13-year-old to squeeze in.

But there was a window.

Artie's eyes lit up. It was small but he was certain he could fit through it. Luckily, Artie was short for his age and not particularly wide.

He could slither through the bathroom window easily enough.

And in a second slice of good luck, the key had been left in the window's lock.

He turned it and pushed the window away from him.

It felt extremely stiff, like it had never been used before.

With a grunt, the window opened up. The night air rushed inside the small room.

Artie breathed a little easier with an escape route set up.

Now he knew that he could make a quick exit if it was needed. It helped to keep his nerves under control.

He took a final deep lungful of the cool night air and moved out of the toilet into the utility room once more.

Quickly and quietly, he scooted through the empty kitchen and pressed himself against the kitchen's island, which was created to be a breakfast bar but lacked the usual cluster of stools.

It was a square room filled with the usual household equipment – sink, cooker, cupboards and a dishwasher.

Over the sink stood the large window that cast light into the garden. Two wooden doors stood in front of him.

One was ajar and looked like it led into a small, dark pantry.

The other door was closed and that was where he could hear voices beyond.

They were still muffled so he would have to get closer if he wanted to overhear their conversation.

He began to move silently across the kitchen.

Years of pretending to be a kick-ass ninja as a youngster had paid off – his well-worn soccer trainers did not make a sound as they padded across the stone tile floor.

Seconds later, Artie found himself pressed against

the second door.

He could not see through the wood but he was now close enough to understand the conversation in the room beyond.

"Berry is upstairs. He will be down in a moment."

It was the same deep voice Artie had heard when he was in the garden earlier. It sounded like a big dog.

The woman replied with a snap: "Tell him to hurry up. We do not have much time and there is still plenty to do."

The conversation abruptly stopped. Artie guessed that the group were waiting in silence for this Berry fella to return.

While he waited, he looked around the kitchen again. It was clean but oddly spotless. It was almost like it had never been used.

Artie's own house was a wonderful mish-mash of tidy and chaos: opened cereal packets on the side, tea-towels strewn over racks, music playing and piles of opened letters everywhere.

This place was completely different.

It had nothing at all – apart from a shiny blue kettle and a sparkling silver bread bin.

There was nothing else.

Artie could feel the hairs on his arms begin to rise. Something told him this was not right.

It was like no-one lived in this house.

This was not a home.

No family lived here – unless they were the tidiest people in the history of the world.

This house was something different.

A ripple of fear swept through him as he realised exactly where he was.

He had stepped into the monsters' lair.

4. SECRETS

It remained quiet on the other side of the door.

Artie pushed himself as close to the keyhole as he dared.

The boy was ready.

He remained crouched and was set to spring towards the toilet window at the first sign of danger.

The door was still closed. Artie could not see into the room – which he guessed was the house's dining room – but he could hear the conversation clearly.

A cold voice broke the lull. "Ah, Berry. Glad you could join us."

Dog Voice did not sound amused.

"I … err … sorry.…"

Berry – the other male voice that Artie had heard earlier – began to bumble an answer but was swiftly interrupted by Dog Voice.

"Shut up and sit down. We have … 43 minutes and we have much to cover. Let's not waste any more time, shall we?"

It was not a request.

Dog Voice barked out the order and the following few seconds of silence told Artie that no-one wished to disagree with him.

Finally, it was the woman who spoke up.

"Where is Birch?"

Artie wrinkled his nose. These people had really weird names.

"He is coming, Gillian, I assure you.

"Once the final touches to our escape route are complete, he will join us here."

There was a murmur of agreement. It made no sense to Artie.

Dog Voice spoke again.

"The time has come. Our moment has arrived.

"Halloween is our night of the year as you know only too well.

"This year, there can be no mistakes. Not a single one. Our survival depends on it."

No response.

Artie stood transfixed to the spot. He held his breath and waited.

Dog Voice continued: "You all know the terrible events that led us here.

"Last year was our lowest point as a species – and we shall never discuss them again.

"Today is our rebirth. Our kind has fallen a long, long way. Now we are on the rise again."

Artie scrunched up his nose with confusion at the ongoing conversation.

Their kind?

What on earth did he mean by that?

The woman with red hair – who they called Gillian – snorted loudly.

She drawled: "What a marvellous speech, Ridgeon.

"It is truly lovely but a complete and utter waste of our time."

The woman's words seemed as if they were arrows

dipped in poison.

Artie thought she had looked terrifying when she waltzed into the house – and he had been right.

Someone to be feared.

An uneasy pause hung over the dining room for a moment.

But Gillian did not wait for a response.

She snapped: "This meeting was called for three reasons. First, we need to know our exact locations for tonight.

"Secondly, where is this new toy that you have boasted about for the best part of a year?

"And finally, we need to know where and when will we meet up again."

There was a loud thud on the table.

Artie pushed against the crack of the door but it was useless – he could not see what had caused the bang.

Berry, who had hardly spoken since the meeting began, piped up: "She is right, Ridgeon.

"Time is against us.

"We need to know the details in full if we are to avoid a repeat of last year's disaster."

Silence again. Artie guessed this Ridgeon character was weighing up the requests.

Finally, he spoke.

His voice was little more than a whisper – icy and firm.

"I understand the need for haste but Birch has still to arrive. I don't want to repeat myself.

"However, apart from sorting our future meeting arrangements, Birch knows the plan in full."

Artie could feel his muscles begin to tighten even further.

His palms were covered with sweat.
Who were these people?
And what on earth was this secret plan they had?

5. NOSEBLEEDS

A jolt of panic swept through Artie. He twisted to look behind him and, much to his relief, the kitchen stood empty and still.

His heart was thumping so loud that it felt like it could erupt from his chest at any moment.

The boy turned back to the conversation behind the door but he kept one ear listening for the dreaded sound of someone else arriving.

Unaware that someone was listening to every word they spoke, the heated conversation in the dining room continued.

Gillian's voice was beginning to rise with anger.

She screeched: "We now have … only 41 minutes to go, Ridgeon! This is YOUR timetable, you fool!

"We are wasting precious time! Tell us what we need to know. You are putting our lives at risk!"

"Oh, don't be so dramatic, Gillian! Everything has been planned perfectly," Ridgeon snapped back, although his deep voice remained in control.

"Indeed, there is a very good reason why Birch will arrive here in the darkness. His location must be kept secret – so moving at night is the only choice if we wish to avoid detection. Now shut up and sit down before you say something you may regret."

A chill ran through his words.

That was not a threat. It was a promise.

Ridgeon continued calmly: "On the map, I have marked out the four houses in the town.

"This is, of course, my house. If anything goes wrong, everyone must return here at once and we will disappear immediately. However, I am certain nothing will go wrong this time around. Our set up is perfect."

Artie heard a loud grunt of agreement from one of the people in the room. He guessed it was Berry.

"Gillian, your house is the furthest away in the centre of Givern Close – sitting on a large junction near the school.

"Berry, you will have this large newly built house on Flamingo Drive near to the sports centre.

"Birch will take the old mansion on High Road. His property will no doubt be the most popular, next to the usual community Halloween celebrations."

Artie memorised the addresses as he listened. He repeated them over and over in his mind.

Givern, Flamingo, High.

Givern, Flamingo, High.

Givern, Flamingo, High.

Gillian's high-pitched drawl shattered Artie's concentration.

"Very well, very well," she replied with a huff. "But how do we lure the children into our so-called perfect trap?"

Ridgeon clicked his fingers.

"A good question, my dear.

"You are right: there can be no repeat of the fiasco

that we experienced last year.

"With this in mind, I have taken extra care to ensure we steal exactly the right type of children we need."

Artie stopped listing the addresses in his head.

His body began to shake a little with fear as he pressed even closer to the door.

He guessed the three of them were hunched over the large table, looking at some sort of map but he could not be sure.

Ridgeon was still talking: "We cannot afford mistakes this time. We are too weak.

"We must get this right or it is all over.

"First, we need to the right type … of children.

"Obviously they must not be teenagers. As poor Herman discovered, their imagination is too narrow by that age.

"They are beginning to think like adults. By then, the precious magic is already slowly disappearing from their minds."

Gillian interrupted. "But not all of them. And capturing a teenager is better than nothing. Or have you forgotten how we survived?"

Ridgeon sighed. "That is true. You are right on both counts.

"Some teens will be more imaginative than others – but how will we know the difference? A teenager is better than nothing, of course. That is a situation I don't want to even consider happening again.

"But, ideally, we need to steal children with vivid imaginations.

"True, some teenagers may possess what we need but many simply will be too grown up."

Berry croaked out a response. With his big eyes

and flabby neck, Artie had a sudden vision of a large toad speaking.

"The people with the best imaginations are kids.

"Surely grabbing a load of little kids will be easiest? The smaller they are, the easier it will be?"

There was a loud bang. It sounded like a fist had smashed down on to the table.

Ridgeon could barely contain his anger as he replied: "No! Listen and stop interrupting.

"This is not a debate. I am telling you what will happen – nothing more.

"Young children are no good either.

"They have plenty of imagination, obviously, and would be perfect for our appetites.

"But they are always accompanied by busy-body parents, which makes them untouchable. Unless one happens to luckily fall into our trap by chance, then parents make them off limits.

"If we wish to remain undetected, we will need to stay clear of them.

"That's why we need to target kids aged between 10 and 12. They're old enough to be trick-or-treating on their own but will still have those juicy imaginations that we can feast upon."

Sounding calmer now, Ridgeon cleared his throat before continuing.

"Each house will have a handful of impressive Halloween decorations but nothing to make them stand out from the crowd too much.

"It is the pumpkins that will attract people to our doors – and into our carefully laid trap.

"And, to avoid a repeat of last year's disaster, we need to ask the all-important question: do they suffer nosebleeds?"

6. GOBLINS

Artie pulled a face. Nosebleeds? What a strange question to ask, he thought to himself.

What was going on?

The kitchen had grown darker as the last light of the October day faded away.

Artie was unsure how long he had been in the house but he could not risk checking the time and accidentally making a noise.

The house was nearly pitch black.

Even in the dining room, the light was dimmed. When he had been standing in the garden, the glare had seemed so bright.

Yet now, the light escaping through the door frame was minimal.

Gillian spoke again: "Yes, a sensible move.

"So, you think Birch's theory is correct then?

"Any child who has regular nosebleeds has already had their imagination removed?"

Ridgeon answered immediately.

"Yes, I do. Our brothers and sisters are spread

across the country – indeed the world. We all need the same thing.

"Nosebleeds are a clear sign that one of our own kind has beaten us to it and their imaginations have already been removed."

Ridgeon sighed loudly. There was a scraping sound as he pushed the chair backwards and stood upright.

"Humans really are simple creatures.

"Even now they think goblins are green, ugly and lack their intelligence. How little they know! I wonder what they would say if they found out that we live beside them in everyday life!"

Laughter filled the room.

Berry croaked: "Humans are so arrogant. They like to imagine creatures like orcs and ghouls – without realising that goblins do exist and have been on this planet for as long as they have. What fools!"

Ridgeon snorted. "Yes, our race is far superior to humans. We know this to be true.

"Centuries ago, our ancestors lived in caves and shunned the daylight. As you know, humans discovered them and our species was hunted to the point of extinction. Now the humans think we only exist in films.

"But we have changed – far quicker than the human race has evolved.

"The changes in the last 50 years mean we now look like them and outsmart them at every turn.

"Once the final flaw in our design is removed, the process that started years ago will finally be complete."

Artie had no idea what he was talking about. Goblins didn't exist, did they? Or was that ghouls? Or vampires?

Artie loved to read but in-depth knowledge about space battles and football stories were not going to be much help here.

The lead goblin continued: "One day we will be able to challenge them – but at the moment there are not enough of us.

"And we need to stop depending on the humans. Until we find a different source of food for survival, our futures will always be locked together.

"But we cannot concern ourselves with this at the moment. That is for another time. Today is the day that we begin to fight back.

"It is Halloween. The night of the Pumpkin Code. An evening when everyone dresses as ghosts, witches and goblins – for fun."

Berry let out a rasping snigger. Ridgeon ignored the interruption and continued.

"You will both find huge pumpkins outside the houses.

"Light them up and you will be part of The Pumpkin Code.

"Children will come to your house willingly because of the Pumpkin Code – asking whether you want to trick or treat. Well, the trick will be on several of them this year.

"When they ring the doorbell, you need to see if they are suitable.

"Are they aged between 10 and 12?

"Do they have parents or adults with them?

"Also, you need to consider whether they are on their own. It would not be wise to tackle a group of two youngsters or more.

"If they are not suitable, give them a sweet, smile and send them merrily on their way.

"If they fit our requirements, invite them inside.

"And that is where our little box of magic will come into play. Simply ask them to delve into the box … and the yellow haze will do the rest as soon as the greedy little imps dive in.

"The haze will collect their imaginations without them even realising what has happened. We only have limited stocks so do not waste any. Guard it with your lives.

"Once it is done, send them on their way quickly, bring the pumpkin inside, shut up the house and return here. We can then share out the feast between us."

A loud thud suddenly made Artie jump.

He twisted around to detect the source of the noise.

The kitchen remained empty behind him.

Artie forced himself to breathe deeply.

This was serious. These people were evil or crazy.

Perhaps they were both.

He needed to tell someone about them – definitely his mum and probably the police too.

They wanted to steal children.

A second noise made Artie turn back towards the dining door.

He realised the sound had been the dining room's patio doors opening and closing.

The sudden rush of air popped the kitchen door open a fraction.

No-one bothered to get up and close it. Perhaps they had not even noticed, but it meant Artie could now see into the room through the narrowest of cracks.

Someone else had joined the gang of goblins.

The boy heard Ridgeon speak again.

"Ah Birch. Is everything ready?"

A man's voice replied with a quiet, deadly whisper.

Unable to stop it, Artie felt a tiny shiver of fear. He could not yet see the newcomer but his voice sounded cruel, tinged with evil.

"I have done everything that was requested. The escape is complete as discussed. No-one will see us leave when the time comes.

"Why have you started without me?"

Silence.

Artie realised that he was not the only person to be afraid of this Birch character.

Ridgeon though appeared unruffled. He replied calmly: "Birch, we have not started anything.

"As you well know, this year we have to stick to the plan.

"Everything has been plotted down to the tiniest detail. We would never let our hunger ruin the biggest night of the year!"

Birch stepped further into the room, moving around the table with heavy, clumping footsteps.

Then he appeared in Artie's eyeline

He was huge.

Dressed in a long dark coat that struggled to cover his enormous shoulders, Birch was at least twice the size of the others.

He pushed his long dark hair out of his eyes to reveal a skull and crossbones earring, which gave Artie the creeps.

A giant arm decorated with a fading snake tattoo pushed the bizarre collection of sunglasses to one side of the table.

Once enough space had been cleared, Birch

dumped several coils of thick wire on to the wooden surface.

Satisfied that the wire was secure, he turned his attentions back to the group. His words remained little more than a whisper.

"I am delighted to hear that the plan is ready and everyone understands the importance of this evening.

"And I congratulate you, Ridgeon, on this entire operation. I really do. However, I have one simple question for you."

Ridgeon raised an eyebrow: "Yes, of course. What is it?"

Birch put two hands on the table and leaned forwards.

His piercing gaze did not settle on anyone in the room though. Instead, he looked directly at Artie.

"Why then is there a strange boy in the kitchen behind you, listening intently to every word you say?"

7. FLEE

For a split second, Artie froze as Birch's glare burned into him. Had he heard correctly? How could this guy possibly know?

The shock only lasted the fraction of a moment. They knew he was there. He had to get out.

He needed to escape these people.

Right now.

He turned in panic and half fell across the stone kitchen floor towards his escape route via the toilet window.

Metres behind him, the dining room door was yanked open.

Light spilled into the dark kitchen.

Artie heard a roar of anger as Ridgeon saw him vanish into the downstairs toilet.

He slammed the door shut and twisted the small lock. It would not hold them for long but it would hopefully give him enough time.

Artie leapt upwards and thrust the top half of his wiry body through the open window.

Earlier he had been convinced that he could fit through it with ease. Now he was not so sure.

By now, his head and shoulders were dangling outside the house but his hips were too big to slip easily through the small gap.

He could hear the goblins trying to force open the toilet door behind him.

Artie began to panic. Birch would easily rip the door off its hinges in seconds. He was almost out of time.

Frantically wiggling his hips through the rectangular window was beginning to work.

Slowly but surely, he was inching free.

"I've got the key to the back door! He will not get very far. Let me through!"

Artie blocked out Gillian's dramatic wailing and concentrated on freeing himself from the clutches of the toilet window.

With a final groan, Artie's hips finally squeezed through the frame. His legs and feet swiftly followed.

"Arrgghhh!"

The boy crashed head first on to the grass in the garden.

He was free.

In a flash, Artie bounced to his feet and shook his head to clear it.

The garden gate stood to his left but he could clearly see the shadow of Gillian trying to unlock the kitchen door.

Within a second or two, she would be outside and cut off his escape.

Instead Artie turned right towards the bushes that had led him here.

With a surge of hope, he realised that the

undergrowth would lead him back to his own garden.

And safety.

He turned the corner but stopped immediately and fell into a crouch.

The hulking figure of Birch was emerging from the patio doors at the far end of the house.

Enemies to the left and enemies to the right. They were also behind him.

This was not good.

Artie's breathing became ragged.

The voice inside of his head was screaming: "You're going to get caught. Move!"

Artie shook his head in response to his inner voice.

There was only one direction left for him to go.

He looked ahead.

On his left, past the gate, was the wall for the garage.

It connected to a fence about ten metres away.

The garden fence was tall and ran between the garage and the bushes. A small shed sat in the far corner.

Artie could not see whether there was a way through the bushes near the shed but he did not have time to explore.

It wasn't an option.

He made up his mind.

Then he ran as fast as he could.

Every ounce of Artie's attention was fixed upon the shed.

Behind him, he was only vaguely aware of the back door to the house being thrown open and his pursuers tumbling out into the darkness.

Gillian wailed: "There he is! Look, there the little

rat goes!"

Artie ignored her.

One of them – he guessed it was Birch – was close enough to hear his breathing.

He hit the shed at full speed.

With a huge leap, Artie's hand shot out and grabbed the felt roof as his trainers pushed against the shed's tiny window ledge.

It worked.

His speed helped him mount the roof with ease.

Artie did not look back. He kept going.

"Nooooo!"

Gillian squealed in anger as the boy who knew their secrets slipped over the shed and out of sight.

8. HUNTED

Thorns scratched at Artie's clothes.

His skin felt like thousands of tiny daggers were being plunged into it every time he tried to move, even through his jeans.

The bush had cushioned his jump from the shed roof – but now it took revenge and ambushed the intruder as he tried to flee its clutches.

Ignoring the pain flowing through his arms and legs, Artie wrenched himself free of the mass of thorns and looked around.

His legs felt wobbly and his body sore but he could not stop and rest now.

Behind him, he could hear Ridgeon barking out instructions.

"Go around both sides and make it quick."

He was not free yet.

The race was not over.

Artie pulled out his phone as he stumbled across the dark garden.

He had to message Fitch.

His friend needed to know that it wasn't safe for her and Stanley to go out tonight. And she would be able to get help.

His thumbs flew over the touchscreen.

"Don't go tonight. Not safe. In trouble. Back soon."

Inevitably, Fitch would think he was joking. He just hoped she would understand that he meant the words.

No kisses. No emojis. No jokes.

Hopefully she would realise he was being serious. She had to.

Artie shoved the phone back into the pocket of his jeans and carefully surveyed the silent garden in front of him.

There was no light coming from inside the house. His heart sank as he realised there was probably no-one home.

Almost instantly Artie knew that he would not find any safety here.

But he had to try.

A twig snapped in the undergrowth not too far behind him.

They were coming through the bushes at the far end of the garden.

Time was short.

In the darkness, Artie stumbled towards the large patio doors and banged on the glass.

"Help! Help me! Please."

No-one came out.

No light switched on in the house in response to the boy's desperate pleas.

His gut instinct had been right: there was no-one

home.

He would not find any help here.

A gate rattled in the distance.

Moments later, the undergrowth at the far end of the garden rustled as someone clumsily made their way through it.

Enemies approached on both sides.

He had no choice: he had to move on.

Artie ducked down and tried to stay in the shadows as he moved towards the next fence.

It was dark but the lights in the street outside cast a yellow glow in part of the garden.

There was no shed here though. Just a strong wooden fence that loomed large above Artie's head.

To make things even worse, in front of the fence was another dense thicket of thorns.

Artie took in a big gulp of oxygen and let it out slowly.

He thought to himself: "Think! Come on, Eason, think! The answer has got to be right in front of you."

The gate rattled again.

It was louder this time.

They were coming.

Artie turned around and half expected to see the monsters bearing down upon him.

But the garden remained empty.

For now.

Yet, as he turned back to the fence and panic threatened to overwhelm him, the solution appeared out of nowhere.

Three wheelie bins stood in the corner.

Without a second thought, he bounded over to the row of bins and tested their strength.

The brown one was filled to the brim with garden

waste, making it easily sturdy enough to hold his weight.

Artie vaulted on to the bin lid and stood looking into the darkness of the next garden.

No light fell in this part of the garden.

An eerie yellow glow lit up the far side of the next garden.

But the area directly in front of him was pitch black.

The houses were too close together and blocked out the light from nearby lamp posts.

Artie hesitated. The thought of getting tangled deep in thorns again did not bother him.

But he did not even know how far the drop was. And there was a faint sound of gurgling that he could not place either.

If the drop was much deeper than he imagined, he could easily break an ankle and then he really would in trouble.

He pulled out his phone again and his finger flicked to open the flashlight.

As he did so, a female voice shrieked only a few metres away from him.

"There he is! Look, he is standing on the bin in the corner. Quick! Grab him, Berry, before he goes over again!"

Artie did not have time to open the phone and check what lay on the other side of the fence.

Time had run out.

He had no other choice.

He shoved the phone back into his pocket and jumped into the darkness.

9. SPLASH

The unseen water was ice cold.

"Arrgggghhh!"

Artie yelped with shock as he plunged up to his waist into freezing water.

The darkness had hidden a garden fish pond.

And the gurgling sound that Artie had heard moments earlier had been the pond's pump.

Artie cursed.

He should have known the sound – they had a similar one in the garden of their old house a couple of years ago.

It was cold and foul-smelling.

Artie bounced on his toes as his teeth began to chatter uncontrollably. He felt like someone had punched him in the stomach and stolen the air from his lungs.

He tried to gulp in mouthfuls of air – but the water felt like it was sucking all the life out of him.

He gritted his teeth.

"It is only a pond," he reminded himself as he

began to wade through the black ripples to the far side.

Feeling the way ahead with his hands, he quickly found the rocky edge of the pond and began to haul his body out.

He had only been in the water for a matter of seconds but he was wet through.

His body screamed for the warmth of the night.

It was hardly boiling hot in the autumn night – but it was certainly a lot warmer than being stuck in the murky depths of the pond.

With an almighty heave, Artie pushed himself completely clear of the water.

He lay alongside the rocky edge, gasping for breath in his sodden clothes.

Artie's heart flipped.

His phone.

In his rush to escape, he had shoved it into one of his pockets and leapt the fence.

He knew it would be ruined if he had rammed it into his jeans.

His shaking fingers groped around his coat … before he breathed a massive sigh of relief.

He had stuck his phone in the breast pocket of his coat.

Artie patted it gently, reassured that – by pure chance – he had kept the device safe. At last, a small slice of luck had fallen in his favour.

A nearby gate rattled. Artie groaned and rolled over. When were they ever going to give up?

The voice in his head answered: "They are not giving up. You know their secret and they do not want anyone to mess up their plans. You heard them, they are crazy.

"You have to get out here now. These people will not stop until they've silenced you."

Panic swept through him again. The voice in his head was right, he knew.

This was real.

There was no time-out or the opportunity to walk away.

They would not stop coming until they had got hold of him – and that was something he could not let happen.

This fear gave him a fresh surge of energy to clamber to his feet.

Artie took a second to consider his new surroundings before beginning to move in a crouch towards the house.

There was no way that he wanted to be caught by these people.

Or goblins. Or whatever the hell they were.

His jeans stuck to him and weighed him down with the extra water they held but he kept moving across the neatly cut lawn.

There were no lights coming from inside this house either.

His heart sank again. He should have guessed.

It belonged to another family that was probably out together enjoying the town's famous Halloween celebrations.

There was no point knocking on the window or calling for help.

No-one sits in the dark in their house at 6pm in October, do they?

Besides, he did not want to give away his position to those following behind. He had made that mistake a few moments earlier and nearly paid the price.

He needed to be clever – and giving away his position every time he reached a house was not the brightest thing to do.

Artie knew that he needed to move on with as little fuss as possible.

Keep quiet, keep moving and keep ahead of them, he told himself.

"Good plan. Now stick to it," replied the voice inside his head.

As he approached the far side of the garden, the street light began to seep through and allowed Artie to see ahead.

It was then he saw him. A large, hulking shape to Artie's right was heading directly towards him.

There were barely five metres between them and the gap was closing fast.

But the light had given the attacker away in the nick of time.

Artie forgot the cold and his soaking wet clothes.

He ran. Out of the corner of his eye, he could tell the man was huge: it could only be Birch.

Artie did not look again. He did not need to. Birch was almost on top of him, close enough to smell his awful aftershave.

Artie knew he would be caught when he reached the fence.

There looked to be no easy way to clamber over this one.

His plan was simple: he would run full pelt at the wooden barrier and try to scramble over it before the goblin could haul him back.

It was hopeless.

They were already too close. They had caught him.

10. BURN

Artie was five metres away from the next fence as he felt the man reach out to grab him.

A quick swerve saw the outstretched hand miss its target and grab nothing but thin air.

Different footsteps pounded in his ears too as the rest of the pursuers closed in.

Artie's legs could not go any faster. He braced himself to try to fight off the next attempt to grab him.

Then, without warning, the house's ultra-bright security lamp sprang into action.

The powerful beam blasted out from the direction of the house and bathed the square garden in artificial light.

"Arrrrgggggghhhhh!"

The nearby footsteps came to an abrupt halt.

And then the screaming began.

Artie wanted to look behind to see what had caused such agony.

But he did not.

He kept moving.

Artie hit the fence with his right foot, while

travelling at top speed.

His arms scrambled to get a grip on the top of the wooden panel.

Further behind him, Ridgeon's booming voice barked out.

"Get out of the cursed light and back into the undergrowth, you fool!

"Quickly now – before the damage becomes too serious!

"Gillian, get the medical box from the front bedroom. I'll bring him back to the house!"

Artie ignored the older man: he was not shouting at him anyway.

He was focused only on the fence.

It was solid and held his light frame with barely a groan.

Within seconds, his hands had gripped the top of the panel and his sodden feet pushed him over the fence to the temporary safety of the next garden.

Yet Artie did not jump off this time.

He had learned from his earlier mistake with the pond.

Instead he lowered himself down carefully.

As he did so, he took a fleeting look backwards into the garden that he had just escaped from.

The security light on the house wall was still blasting its ultra-powerful rays into the October night sky. The entire garden was lit up like daytime.

In the undergrowth running along the bottom of the garden, Artie could see a figure crouched over another person, who looked much bigger than the first.

Birch.

Out of the group, only Birch was that big. Artie's

heart leapt.

Somehow he had managed to bring down the giant without even trying.

It was a complete mystery but it was quite clear that Birch had been badly hurt. The howls of agony had told Artie that.

The big brute was sitting in the darkest corner of the garden – a metre or so away from the powerful rays of light.

Ridgeon was bent over him, also out of the lamp's light.

The pair of goblins disappeared behind the wooden fence as Artie let himself slowly drop down into the next garden.

He landed with as little noise as possible.

His mind raced as he considered the events of the last few moments.

This crazy gang had nearly caught him. Birch had almost been upon him when he began to scream like a wild animal.

But what had hurt the giant so badly?

The light? Surely not.

They had used light in the house and they were happy to walk around in daylight.

Why would this suddenly hurt them?

Artie did not know the answers.

Whatever had happened, it showed that they had a weakness.

These fiends were not invincible.

They could be stopped.

Completely by accident, he had somehow discovered a weak point. Ridgeon's reaction to the light had been a giveaway.

Unfortunately, Artie did not know exactly what

that weakness was yet.

But it was still an opportunity.

They could be hurt.

Birch was huge – a terrifying beast with hands like shovels and a tree trunk-sized neck.

His long hair and abnormal size made him look like some of the wrestlers that Artie and Stanley watched every week on the telly.

Yet he had screamed with agony for no apparent reason.

Why?

Artie shivered.

His wet clothing stuck to him as the autumn temperatures began to drop for night.

He realised his teeth had been chattering again as he mulled over the situation.

Artie knew he needed to get out of these wet clothes.

With three of the goblins heading back to their hideaway, there was only one of their gang standing between him and freedom.

Berry.

Artie stood up. The chase was nearly over.

He could see there were two more houses to go before he would reach the safety of the main road.

But he was on the home straight.

A minute or two and he would be away from these monsters.

Birch would not be able to chase him again so that meant the undergrowth route was now free.

No more fences.

Or ponds.

Or nasty surprises.

Artie knew these woods better than anyone else in

the town.

He would disappear into the darkness – and then he would decide how to tackle these evil creatures.

Barely making a sound, he moved across the garden and passed carefully into the bushes on his right.

The boy did not see the shadowy figure slip through the gate and moments later silently follow him into the undergrowth.

11. BAD TIMING

As soon as the darkness of the woods surrounded him, Artie felt instantly more at ease.

He moved towards a dark part of the wood and took a moment to get his bearings.

These were his woods.

He had trodden these paths more than anyone he had ever met.

He knew almost every twist and turn.

It looked quite different in the dark but Artie did not panic.

It was certainly easier finding his way through here than wading through garden ponds and vaulting tall wooden fences.

He cringed as he thought about the poor people who would return home from trick or treating to find their gardens wrecked by the chase.

But he would happily own up.

His story might sound like a crazy load of make-believe to those people but it was the truth. They would have to believe him eventually.

His mum would understand. She always did.

All he had to do was get back to her and Stanley.

His house.

His family.

His friends.

Crack.

A twig snapped some distance behind him.

Artie froze.

Someone was close by.

His daydreaming stopped in a flash.

He dropped down on to his haunches and peered into the gloom where the sound had come from.

Nothing moved.

But the sound was definitely made by something that was alive.

Artie strained all his senses to try to detect the new danger.

He had lost track of time – he had no idea if this game of hide-and-seek had lasted for an hour or a couple of minutes.

But he was focused on one single thing: staying alive.

Apart from the trees swaying gently in the breeze, it was quiet.

He could not smell anything except from decaying leaves on the ground and the foul stench of the pond that still clung to him.

The darkness only allowed him to see about three or four metres in any direction.

Everything looked still.

Despite his wet clothing, Artie could feel a trickle of sweat run down his back.

His mind raced over the options.

Should he move?

Or should he wait it out?

The faint sound of a car helped to make up his mind.

As the car travelled along the street, its engine provided enough noise for Artie to move without giving his position away.

Soon though the vehicle's noise dwindled as the driver speed off.

With his cover gone, Artie moved away from the muddy footpath and crouched beside an ancient-looking tree.

Now the end of the undergrowth was only about 30 metres away.

He had nearly made it.

Once he was out on the road, it was only a matter of minutes before he would be home.

These goons surely wouldn't want to abduct him on a busy street.

Crack.

Another sound came from behind him.

This one was nearby.

Much closer.

Artie pressed himself against the hefty tree trunk and hoped to stay as invisible as possible.

Then he saw him.

Berry.

Treading carefully, the goblin picked his way through the woodland methodically – like a predator hunting prey.

He was close – perhaps five metres away.

Artie watched Berry's head moving from side to side as he looked for signs of his quarry.

Four metres.

Three metres.

He stank. The reek of onions made Artie want to retch.

Instead, he suffered the stench in silence. He took a silent breath in and held it.

Two metres.

They were level – probably a metre or less between them.

Berry stopped. His eyes scanned the undergrowth around him.

Artie did not dare to breathe, despite his lungs beginning to scream for air. If he did, he knew he would be caught.

The hunter stood almost on top of his prey but still he could not see him. He paused for 30 seconds, although the delay seemed to take longer in Artie's mind.

Finally, Berry began to move again.

The dirt track began to twist away from Artie's position – and Berry followed the path deeper into the woodland.

Seconds later, the monster disappeared from Artie's view and the boy allowed himself to release the gulp of air that he had held for so long.

That had been close.

Too close.

But somehow Artie had still evaded their wicked clutches.

His plans though needed to change again.

With Berry now ahead of him, it meant the woodland escape was no longer an option.

But it also meant that the garden gates were no longer being watched.

He could cut back into one of the gardens, jump over the gate, run up the cul-de-sac and join the road towards his house.

Artie's heart leapt with joy.

His chance had come.

Escape was still within touching distance.

And then the unthinkable happened.

Something was wrong.

Artie looked downwards, his stomach filling rapidly with fear.

His phone began to ring.

12. THE HOLE

Time seemed to slow to a crawl.

But everything was still happening far too quickly for Artie.

Before the smartphone even made a sound, the strong vibrations against his chest told him what was coming.

Aghast at the terrible timing, Artie delved into his pocket to grab the phone and cancel the call before it gave him away.

Even as he yanked it free from his jacket pocket, he knew it was too late.

The familiar sounds of his favourite band began to fill the night air. It was not loud but that did not matter.

In the near silence, the sound would carry much further than normal.

Berry would hear it and know exactly where he was.

He glanced at the smartphone's screen.

Fitch.

She never rang him.

Ever.

He grimaced.

This was his fault.

The desperate message he had sent earlier must have worried his friend enough into giving him a call.

Instead of helping him though, she had made the situation a hundred times worse.

A quick flick of his thumb rejected the incoming call.

The phone went silent.

Yet the damage had already been done. Danger was close at hand.

Artie clutched the phone in his hand in case Fitch decided to ring back.

He needed to make a move quickly.

The garden gate exit plan remained the best option, but the problem was that he did not know where Berry was.

Artie peered through the gloom in the direction he planned to escape.

The route looked clear, although his vision was restricted by the dark.

Artie took a deep breath and left the cover of the tree trunk, heading towards the gardens once more.

The hand grabbed him before he could even begin to run at full speed.

"Gotcha, little rabbit. Where do you think you are heading off to?"

Berry grabbed Artie by the scruff of the neck and lifted him off the ground with ease.

Artie's eyes widened with terror. He never would have guessed that Berry could be so strong.

The goblin only looked slight, perhaps even a

touch wimpy. Yet Artie had been picked up like a rag doll.

The goblin grinned, revealing a mouthful of horrible black teeth: "You have caused us a lot of trouble, boy, and now you are going to pay the price."

Artie's heart skipped a beat.

He remembered the discussions earlier and knew exactly what Berry wanted: his imagination.

He kicked his legs to try to escape the monster's clutches but they merely flailed in mid-air, useless.

Berry kept Artie at arm's length so he could not lash out as he began to carry his prize back towards the house.

The usual voice inside Artie's head roared at him: "Think, Eason, think!"

Artie knew this would be his best opportunity to get away.

Once Berry had joined up again with the others, he would be outnumbered at least three to one.

Perhaps four to one, if Birch had recovered from the accident earlier.

Birch.

Suddenly Artie knew what to do.

He kept his hands down by his side but his fingers crawled into his pocket.

Without looking downwards, his thumb flicked his phone open.

He knew how the phone worked inside out and unlocked the device with minimal effort.

The screen immediately flashed into life, casting a small patch of light on the ground as they moved along the muddy path.

Artie stole a glance at Berry.

He was looking directly ahead – fully focused on

taking his prize to the rest of his tribe.

The pair of them were moving at a fast pace along the woodland track.

The garden with the security light was now on their right.

It had switched off again.

He guessed the others had retreated back to the original house by now.

Artie felt Berry's pace begin to drop.

The goblin had seen the light from Artie's phone.

"Where's that coming from …?"

Berry did not get the chance to finish the sentence.

With a swift look at the screen as he brought the phone to head height, Artie switched on the flashlight.

The power of the screen's glare immediately trebled, sending bright rays of light into the night.

He twisted and plunged the phone under Berry's nose.

As the goblin was holding Artie, he could not use his arms to block the searing light from flooding directly into his face.

He screamed in agony.

They fell together.

Downwards they tumbled, out of sight and far away from the houses.

They came to rest in a heap in a deep hole, which was surrounded by dying brambles and bushes.

Berry's fingers rushed to protect his face.

His other hand still clung like a pincer to Artie's neck.

The pair rolled on the muddy floor – the goblin still thrashing wildly as the phone's rays stayed near his skin.

Eventually, the pain became too much.

Berry released Artie from his vice-like grip and put both hands over his face.

Free from his clutches, Artie pushed himself off the goblin but held the phone steady – with the light trained upon his enemy.

There was a strange smell in the air.

It was revolting, a stench that Artie had never smelt before.

Berry continued to writhe and howl on the floor in front of him.

Artie needed answers.

He flicked the flashlight off but kept the phone fixed on his enemy's face in case of any sudden movements.

The phone's screen cast a strange glow over the goblin.

Berry stopped thrashing and lay still.

Slowly the goblin's groaning stopped and finally he lowered his gloved hands.

Then Artie saw Berry's ruined face in the ghostly light.

And immediately he understood why the goblin had shrieked with such pain. It looked like his face had melted.

The boy ignored the ghastly sight beneath him.

He kept the phone close to him in case Berry tried to snatch it away – and remove his weapon.

But Berry did not move.

Artie hissed: "I want to know everything so I can stop your gang from capturing any other innocent kids.

"Now tell me the plan – and make sure you don't miss out a single detail."

Martin Smith

PART TWO

THE CODE

13. HALLOWEEN

Fitch shook her head with frustration.

This was typical Artie. Only her best friend would send a dramatic message – and then divert your call to answerphone.

She angrily pushed her brown fringe out of her eyes and spoke aloud even though she was alone in her bedroom.

"He is such an idiot.

"Does he believe I am some sort of moron? He may be older than me but that doesn't make him any smarter, whatever he thinks."

Short and slender, Fitch only came up to the shoulders of most of the other kids in her school year. Despite her size, no-one dared to ever mess her about – Fitch would never allow it. She was feisty, to say the least.

Artie loved to gloat that he was older by four months. He knew perfectly well that it would wind her up.

At the moment, he was 13 and Fitch was still 12 – and he had never stopped mentioning it since his birthday arrived.

A small voice inside her head urged her to ring him again – just in case.

But she ignored it.

Fitch was certain that he was pulling her leg as usual. Artie was always joking around, playing the fool and winding everyone up.

They had been friends since the early days of primary school.

They were older now but their friendship remained as strong as ever.

Over the years, Fitch had become a part of the Eason household.

With only an adult sister who had left home years ago, Fitch felt like the Eason brothers were her brothers too.

Despite their closeness though, Artie still always managed to wind her up one way or another.

They were such different characters.

Artie was charismatic and daring, full of adventure and risks.

Fitch, on the other hand, was no-nonsense and determined, sensible and straightforward.

Yet the combination between the two of them somehow worked.

There never seemed to be any awkwardness or uncomfortableness between them – they knew each other inside out.

And Artie never stopped trying to wind her up.

It was in his nature.

Today was typical Artie Eason.

Fitch should have seen this coming.

It was Halloween – the evening of mischief, spooky goings-on and scariness across the world.

In short, it was the perfect opportunity for a prankster like Artie to take full advantage.

Fitch did not know why she always fell for his absurd tales.

She could have gone trick or treating with a bunch of other friends but Artie had insisted that she go out with him and Stanley.

His little brother would be disappointed if she wasn't with them, he had explained to her at school.

Fitch had happily agreed to go with them – and they were set to meet at Artie's house at 6.30pm.

It was now 6.20pm and she was going to be late, which was a regular occurrence for her.

But Artie was mainly to blame.

She would give him a dead arm as soon as she saw the little weasel.

First came the over-the-top dramatic message that had arrived while she was in the shower.

"Don't go tonight. Not safe. In trouble. Back soon."

She had fallen for it at first.

Her hands had begun to shake as she read the terrifying wording.

Then she realised: this was Artie. It was bound to be a stupid game of some sort.

So she had tried to ignore it.

But, as he almost certainly knew it would, anxiety began to gnaw away at her until finally she had cracked.

Against her better judgement, she dialled his number – hoping to get some answers from him.

Instead he had diverted her to answerphone.

The little rat.

It was then she realised he was fooling around with her – playing ridiculous mind games purely because it was the scariest night of the year.

Her finger still hovered over the call button.

It had been two minutes since he had decided to reject her call.

Then Fitch finally made up her mind.

Her idiot friend would not win this time.

She was not falling for that joker's stupid games yet again.

"If he thinks that I am falling for his usual pranks, then he is mistaken."

Her thumb flicked her phone closed.

Fitch slipped the device into her pocket and looked down at her brand-new red and blue super hero outfit.

Supergirl did not take any nonsense from other people, why should she?

Fitch sighed.

Artie could play his silly games.

But she would not let Stanley miss out on the ghoulish fun and games.

Halloween only came around once a year and it would be unfair on the little boy not to take him out.

They would go trick or treating together – with Artie or not.

14. OGRE

Stanley flung open the door the moment that Fitch's finger left the buzzer.

"Raaaarrrr!"

Fitch screamed in an over-the-top reaction before bursting into a fit of giggles.

Dressed as a bright green ogre, Stanley looked terrifying – for someone who came up to her elbow.

"I love Shrek! You look so great. Fab costume, Stan the Man!"

Fitch hugged the little boy warmly.

"Thank you, Finny."

Fitch raised her eyebrows and put him back down on the ground.

"Why are we using that name again, Mr Eason?"

Fitch's real name was rarely used.

Her birth certificate called her Finlay Mitchell, which she loathed with a passion.

Only her mum still insisted on using her full name – and it lead to plenty of arguments.

And whenever someone made the mistake to

shorten her name to Fin or Finny, they got such a frosty response they never did it again.

Stanley knew this. He may only have been seven years old but, as Fin knew, he was like his older brother in so many ways.

In short, he was a wind-up merchant.

Stanley laughed: "Sorry Finny … oops, I mean Fitch."

She grabbed the young boy into a playful bear hug and ruffled his hair through his Shrek mask.

"You are a little rascal, Eason!"

She affectionately blew a raspberry on his neck.

"Hey! Put me down!"

Stanley wrestled out of her grip and retreated into the hallway, looking for his shoes.

Fitch stepped into the house and closed the door behind her.

"Hi Fitch! Wow, great outfit – one of my favourite super-heroes! Is Artie with you?"

Stanley and Artie's mum Belinda came into the hallway, wiping her hands on a grubby-looking tea-towel.

"Hi Belinda. Thank you. No, he is not.

"And I have absolutely no idea where he is, I'm afraid."

Belinda puffed out her cheeks. She looked hot and bothered from cooking the family's dinner.

"That boy! He was out in the garden kicking the ball about with Jack and then both of them disappeared!"

Fitch should have known Jack – Artie's regular partner in crime – would be involved somehow. As usual, they were causing trouble together.

Belinda continued talking as she tried to straighten

Stanley's mask while the younger boy battled to escape his mother's clutches.

"I have not heard from my eldest since he went out to play football. His dinner is now completely ruined – I am going to string him up when I get hold of him!"

Fitch felt a pang of uncertainty.

Artie never missed food – ever. Even when he was in hospital once, he still ate the awful meals.

But if he had been in real trouble, he would have answered her phone call, wouldn't he?

And he was with Jack, after all.

She reminded herself: "This is all a big joke. Don't worry his mum any more. She has enough to cope with."

Fitch gently placed a hand on Belinda's shoulder.

"He messaged me earlier.

"I think your son may well be planning a Halloween surprise for me and someone else we know."

She nodded in Stanley's direction.

They both looked at the younger boy, who was not listening to their conversation. He had finally managed to escape his mum's attentions and was busy pulling on his trainers.

Belinda shook her head.

"Tell him that he's in big trouble when he gets home. I could wring his neck sometimes!"

Fitch knew Artie's mum well enough to know her rage was beginning to die down.

If she thought Artie was doing something for his little brother, her bad mood would soon disappear.

Belinda Eason was a kind woman, who rarely got cross. Fitch marvelled at how she juggled so much –

looking after two boys on her own and keeping two part-time jobs took some effort. Yet she was rarely cross and almost always had a cheerful smile.

Fitch nodded. "OK. I will tell him.

"You know what Artie is like: always joking around."

Belinda rolled her eyes and brushed a stray strand of blonde hair out of her eyes.

"Oh yes. I know only too well. Look, why don't you two head off. Stanley has been itching to get out of here for about the last hour!"

Belinda checked her wrist-watch and blew out her cheeks.

"I am running so late. I have got to get these dishes cleared up, then sort tomorrow's lunches and then get myself ready. Artie is in big trouble when I get hold of him.

"Fitch, I hate to ask but could you take Stanley to the celebrations for me please? I will be along as soon as I have got everything sorted here – hopefully it will only be half an hour or so?"

Fitch smiled warmly. "Of course I will. I was planning to go with you guys anyway. Take as long as you need. We'll have a great time."

Belinda gave her a small hug and then turned to her younger son, who had finally managed to pull on his trainers. He had picked up the plastic toy club that completed his outfit as well as a bright orange pie.

The ogre was ready.

"Raaaarrrr!"

Belinda pretended to scream.

"Stanley Eason, you make a terrific ogre!

"If I hadn't bought those funky trainers myself, I would never have known that was you!

"Try not to scare too many people out there tonight. I am going to meet you guys as soon as I've got all this mess cleared up. Be a good boy for Fitch, OK?"

Stanley nodded eagerly. He gave his mum a quick hug and took Fitch's outstretched hand.

Fitch grinned at Belinda as she opened the front door.

"Give me a ring when you get into town and I'll tell you where we are.

"As for Artie, don't worry. I am sure whatever he has planned, it will be great fun. If I see him before you, I'll warn him that he's in deep trouble."

They said goodbye and Fitch stepped out into the cool autumn air with Stanley next to her.

"Right Stanley. There are three really simple rules for tonight," Fitch spoke as they walked together.

"Rule one: we must hold hands."

Stanley pulled a face and Fitch stopped in her tracks.

"I mean it. I know you're seven but there are going to be loads of people out tonight. I can't lose you or I'll never find you. Understood?"

She thrust her hand out in his direction and waited for Stanley to take hold of it, which he did somewhat reluctantly.

"Rule two: don't talk to strangers – but you know that already, don't you?"

Stanley nodded: "And rule number three?"

Fitch smiled: "That's the easiest one! We must have lots … of fun!"

They laughed together and walked hand-in-hand into the evening with Fitch ignoring the niggles of worry deep inside her stomach.

15. DECISIONS

The Eason house was not too far away from the main Halloween celebrations on the town's recreation ground.

Families from across the region now flocked to Foston every year for Halloween.

What had originally started out as a small community event for the town's residents had evolved into a huge carnival of spooky craziness.

The night air was filled with shrieks, spices and sweet smells: toffee apples, candyfloss and doughnuts.

Rows of stalls boasted some of the most absurd-looking pumpkins imaginable along with apple bobbing competitions and ghoulish games.

Two huge bouncy castles especially decked out in Halloween-themed spider webs towered over one end of the park, blasting out pop music.

Fitch and Stanley arrived at the park's gates and looked across the field that they visited almost every day.

It looked a little different from most years.

As usual there was a sea of people in fancy dress, bright lights, screams and laughter.

But the carnival stalls sat on the opposite side of the park to its normal site.

"Why have they changed the fair's position?" Fitch thought out loud.

A friendly looking man, surrounded by a horde of small cackling witches, overheard Fitch's question and began to answer.

He said: "The meadow is completely flooded. I asked the same question to one of the organisers about half an hour ago."

Fitch pulled a face.

"Flooded? We have not had much rain through October! That is crazy."

The man smiled.

"That's exactly what I said. Apparently, part of the Foston Brook has become all clogged up and no-one realised until it was too late.

"The meadow was completely waterlogged when the stalls and rides began to arrive so they switched the fair to the other side of the park.

"Well, it is nice to have a change now and again, I say."

Being dragged away by his excited crowd of children, the kind stranger waved a quick cheerio and was lost in the crowds of people moments later.

Fitch took a final look at the dark, empty side of the park and caught the reflection of the bright lights shimmering on the surface water.

She had lived in Foston all her life and the meadow had never flooded before. Still, there was a first time for everything.

Fitch turned her attention back on the chaotic

scenes in front of her.

She felt Stanley grip her hand a little harder as they looked at the mass of bodies moving around the park.

The younger boy had been full of bravado on the way to the celebrations – but now he could not hide his nerves.

"Where is Artie?"

This was the first time since they had left the house that Stanley had asked about his older brother.

Fitch felt yet another pang of worry but tried to dismiss it.

"He is bound to be here somewhere, Stanley. It is all part of his game, I think.

"Let's stand here for a moment while I can check my phone and see if he has sent another message.

"Can you do me a favour please?

"I need you to keep on the lookout to spot that great big ratbag of a brother please?"

Stanley nodded eagerly.

His eyes were as large as saucers as he watched the crowds to try to catch a glimpse of his missing big brother.

Fitch smiled to herself. Stanley was such a typical seven-year-old: a bundle of energy, endless questions and enthusiasm.

She smiled at the little boy as she pulled out her phone.

There was no new message.

Ringing Artie again was still an option, but she looked down at Stanley instead.

She could not worry him.

After all, Artie was bound to be kidding around.

She thrust the phone back into her bag.

"Right. Artie will meet us later, Stan the Man.

"I know you want to go on the bouncy castle but I think we should go trick or treating first. OK?"

Stanley shook his head.

"No! I wanna go on the spider's web."

Fitch knew this would happen.

They would queue up for ages and maybe Stanley would get to go on one fair ride or perhaps two.

However she had already planned ahead for the conversation with this in mind.

"OK. It is your choice, Stan, but I am worried about the houses doing trick or treating running out of sweets before we even get there.

"I think we should go trick or treating, fill up your bucket with loads of sweets and then do a couple of the rides on the way home to celebrate.

"What do you think?"

Stanley ran a hand through his short brown hair as he thought through Fitch's plan.

The young boy was torn, she knew. He badly wanted to go on the giant bouncy castles – what kid didn't?

But the thought of having no sweets to take home was a game-changer.

She watched as he looked down at his empty basket and knew he was beginning to sway.

Fitch kneeled down to his height.

"I think we should go right now – and do as many houses as possible.

"The sooner your basket is filled with goodies, the quicker we can hit the rides."

That sealed it.

Stanley nodded eagerly and began walking towards the houses that lined the edge of the park before Fitch had stood up again.

"Come on Fitch! We need to do this quickly! Let's do it!"

Stanley began to run.

Fitch followed with a big grin.

Within a couple of bounds she had caught up with him.

They left behind the noisy bright lights of the fair – and headed towards the bustling streets lined with twinkling pumpkins.

16. THE PUMPKIN CODE

Stanley could not keep the smile from his face.

The streets were alive with people in fantastic costumes – ghosts, witches, warlocks and ghouls paraded up and down in front of them.

And that wasn't all.

Only a few metres away from Fitch and Stanley were superheroes, wrestlers and even Elvis.

The air was alive with laughter and screams of joy – exactly what Halloween was all about.

Young and old alike had taken to the streets to take part in the annual trick or treating event.

Doors were being knocked upon and sweets dished out to delighted children across the town.

Fitch stepped off the kerb into the middle of the road. With so many people outside, there was no danger of cars coming down the road any time soon.

"So where shall we start, Stan the Man?"

Stanley remained on the pavement. With the extra height, he nearly came up to her chin.

"What about…."

Stan paused as he studied the nearby houses. He could never make up his mind about anything.

Fitch waited patiently as the young boy made a decision.

"… that house over there?"

Stanley pointed to the mass of people.

Fitch stood on her tiptoes to see the property he was indicating towards.

It was dark with no-one queuing up outside.

She shook her head.

"No, we can't do that one, silly.

"Look, there's no pumpkin outside!

"Let's try that one over there instead."

Fitch grabbed Stanley's hand and they weaved through the crowds towards a large detached house, which faced the corner of the park.

It was a huge home with a large garden too.

And the people who lived there must really love Halloween.

A smoke machine pumped out fake spooky mist into the garden, which had gravestones and coffins planted across the lawn.

The sounds of Michael Jackson's Thriller boomed out from the direction of the double garage.

Fitch and Stanley joined the queue of children waiting to speak to a green-coloured witch, who was noisily stirring a cauldron outside the front door.

Surrounded by thick smoke and gruesome characters, Fitch was not surprised when Stanley squeezed her hand tightly.

She returned the grip to reassure him – the decorations may have been wonderful but kids could easily get scared, particularly on Halloween.

"Fitch?"

"Yes, Stanley?"

"What do you mean about the pumpkins?"

Fitch rolled her eyes.

"Are you telling me that you don't know about the Pumpkin Code?"

Stanley shook his head.

They moved several steps forward as a group of smiling children left the queue, proudly clutching the sweets they had just been given.

Fitch tutted.

"Your brother is quite possibly the most useless person in the history of the world.

"Make sure you remember to tell him that when we see him, won't you?

"I thought everyone knew about the Pumpkin Code and how it worked. Listen closely because it is really important but also very simple."

Despite all the noise and games happening around them, Stanley stared at Fitch intently.

His eyes, she noticed, were wide open again.

She continued: "We all know that most people love Halloween but there are others who are not too keen."

"Who?"

Stanley seemed genuinely offended by the mere suggestion that anyone could dislike Halloween.

Fitch shrugged. "Some people find it too scary.

"Some older people don't like people knocking on their doors when it is dark.

"And that's fine. It is their choice – no-one has to take part if they don't want to, do they?"

Stanley had a puzzled look.

She recognised that face. It told her that the boy was deep in concentration.

Stanley's eyes lit up: "Like my gran? I bet she doesn't like it?"

Fitch nodded: "Bingo. That is exactly the reason why some clever person somewhere in the world invented the Pumpkin Code.

"It is really simple.

"So, if you have sweets and want people to knock on your door trick or treating, you put a pumpkin on the doorstep.

"Then you light it up and trick or treaters know that they are welcome to knock on your door."

They stepped forward again as two grinning girls dressed as bumblebees turned away from the front of the queue – placing their new goodies into already-full baskets.

Fitch and Stanley were now one away from the front of the queue. They would be next.

Fitch finished the story at top speed.

"It all works rather nicely. The pumpkins line the streets and give the night a spooky look.

"People who don't like Halloween don't put a pumpkin outside their door.

"It means they don't get any hassle or have to spend the evening living in fear, refusing to answer their front doors.

"Those of us who like Halloween – and judging by the amount of people out tonight that is an awful lot of us – know that we are safe to visit any house with a pumpkin outside the door.

"That is the rule of the Pumpkin Code. Never forget!"

17. ALARM

Fitch and Stanley finally reached the front of the queue.

The witch in front of them was obviously enjoying her night.

She beamed at the little boy with a dazzling smile as she pretended to stir the iron pot, which was full of chocolates and other sweet treats.

A smoke machine stopped trick or treaters from being able to see into the huge tub and a red light gave it a ghoulish tinge.

The witch cackled: "Hello my little cherubs.

"Does an ogre and a superhero dare to dip a hand into my delicious cauldron of doom?"

Stanley froze with fear.

Fitch kept hold of the boy's hand and kneeled down beside him.

"Let's do it together."

Stanley nodded but still kept a wary eye on the witch, who was grinning at him.

He obviously wanted the chocolate but did not

particularly want to go anywhere near this witch or her green brew.

Fitch guided Stan's hand over the rim and gently leaned over the edge of the cauldron.

Within seconds, their groping fingers touched a metallic sweet wrapper and they pulled it out with a flourish.

"Yes! Got one!"

Stanley sounded as if he'd won the lottery and quickly plonked the find into his basket in case the woman tried to pinch it back.

The witch laughed at his triumphant look of delight as Fitch calmly scooped out another prize and dumped it into her basket too.

They thanked the witch for her kindness and turned to go.

As they moved away from the cauldron, the witch called after them: "You were lucky, young ones.

"Be careful, out there. Anything can happen at Halloween."

Moments later, they were back on the road.

But Stanley did not let Fitch's hand go until they had left the witch and the spooky garden a long way behind.

Both sides of the road were jam-packed with people. At this rate, they would have to queue for every house.

That wasn't ideal.

Fitch knew Stanley would only be allowed to stay out for an hour or so on a dark school night.

By the time his mum found them, he would be close to heading home.

They had no time to waste.

The older girl guided Stanley carefully through the

bustling crowds.

Artie had taught her how to be successful at trick or treating – always start in the quieter areas and work your way back into the town.

Fitch said clearly: "Come on, Stan.

"This part of the town is a little bit too busy for us so I have a new plan.

"We'll start on the next street, head towards your school, loop back around and do these streets on the way home."

Stanley nodded with excitement.

The pair wound their way through the bustling streets, looking at the strange sights that only Halloween can produce.

With the crowds and the decorations to keep them occupied, neither of them noticed the tall dark shadow with a bright white skull-mask creep up silently behind them.

"Rarrrrrrr!"

Both Fitch and Stanley jumped with fright as the figure dressed all in black pounced on them.

Fitch screamed as she turned around and saw the skull only centimetres from her face.

"Easy, Fitch! It's only me!"

Artie.

The voice was muffled but it had to be him.

Was this really his big surprise?

Fitch lashed out: "You are such an idiot!

"This has not been funny in the slightest.

"Why do you always do this?"

She was incredibly angry, of course, but she also felt relief surge through her as she belted her friend in the tummy.

"Owww!"

This time Fitch immediately knew something wasn't right.

Even though it was still muffled, it was obvious that the voice did not match.

The shadow removed the skull mask.

It wasn't Artie at all.

Fitch screamed.

18. JACK

"Woah, Fitch! What are you doing? Relax. It's only me!"

The mask dropped to the ground as Jack put his hands up in the air in a half-hearted apology. He pushed the long strands of blonde hair out of his eyes and beamed at the pair of them.

He towered above them and his strong arms reminded Fitch of tree trunks.

With his shoulder-length hair, Jack could easily have been mistaken for a professional surfer – except they lived nowhere near the sea.

He was easily the oldest-looking kid in their school year – even if he acted like Stanley's age half the time.

"Gotcha there, didn't I?"

Fitch felt her cheeks begin to burn.

But a quick look over her shoulder revealed there was no need to be embarrassed: it was Halloween and the crisp evening air was filled with plenty of screams and shrieks.

No-one on the busy streets gave the three of them a second glance.

Nonetheless, she still gave Artie's friend a sharp dig in the stomach.

"What are you doing, you idiot! You scared the life out of us. Poor Stanley isn't used to this kind of nonsense."

Jack's smile disappeared. He tried to reply but began to jumble up the words.

"It … was a … joke. I thought it would be … err … pretty funny!"

To be fair, Jack wasn't a practical joker like Artie. He was cool – ultra relaxed and was always smiling. Annoyingly, he was one of those people who seemed to be good at absolutely everything.

Stanley began to chuckle. The small freckles on his button nose disappeared as his face changed into a huge smile.

"You didn't scare me, Jackster!

"It was completely brilliant.

"I knew it was you all along."

Jack laughed at the boy's obvious lie – and played along as he scooped Stan into his arms.

"I noticed, dude. It was only Fitch here who was the big scaredy cat. Luckily, she had you to keep her safe, huh?"

Stanley nodded eagerly and puffed his chest out a little. Jack gave Fitch a wink, but she did not respond. It was clear she was still mad with him.

"Brazier! You coming?"

Hearing his surname, Jack turned back to the large group of boys standing nearby.

Fitch knew most of them from school and nodded a small greeting in their direction.

Jack replied: "Yeah, give me a minute. Head down there and I'll catch you up."

He waved his friends in the direction that Fitch and Stanley had just come from.

The boys shrugged and moved off. Soon they were swallowed up in the dense throng of people.

Jack returned his attention to Fitch and Stanley and flashed his bright white teeth with a big smile.

"Right, where's the big man then?"

Fitch's eyes narrowed. Her face was like thunder and she spoke with coldness: "That is a very good question, Mr Brazier."

Jack pulled a face of surprise.

Fitch continued: "We hoped you might be able to tell us: as you're the last person to have seen him."

Jack let Stan gently slip down to the ground so the younger boy did not overhear the conversation.

He whispered: "What on earth do you mean? I saw him a couple of hours ago when we had a quick kickabout before tea."

Fitch sighed. This whole situation seemed to become more confusing with every minute that passed.

She looked at Jack, trying to understand if he was pulling her leg or not. Was he being serious or was he part of this whole pointless joke?

His face did not flinch. She could not tell either way, so Fitch tried again – in a more direct way.

"So, exactly what was Artie doing when you left him?"

Jack tried to remember what happened earlier in the evening as Fitch's fierce glare continued to burn into him.

He spoke slowly as he remembered: "I had to go … home for dinner. One of my shots went over the fence … and I left Artie to go and get it."

Fitch shook her head.

"So, let me get this straight: you booted the ball over the fence but left your mate to go and get it?

"What a great friend, you are."

Jack winced at the harshness in the words but Fitch did not care if he felt uncomfortable.

The unease in her stomach was back. And it was worse than before.

She leaned in closer towards Jack to stop Stanley overhearing.

The little boy was not interested anyway – he was gawping delightedly at a troop of Ewoks walking by.

Confident the younger boy was concentrating on the gaggle of Star Wars characters rather than their conversation, Fitch whispered: "Artie is missing … and it is your fault."

She regretted the words almost as soon as they left her mouth.

They were too harsh – and came out edged with a spitefulness she did not intend.

Jack's face fell.

He stuttered a reply.

"I … didn't … know. I.…"

He stopped, realising he could not say anything to change the situation.

She was right: it should have been him to retrieve the ball when it disappeared over the fence. Instead he had swanned off home and left his mate to get the ball back. But what could possibly have gone wrong?

Fitch put a hand on his shoulder and pulled out her phone.

"He sent me this a little while ago.

"I thought that idiot was messing around as usual. I still do in a way, I guess."

Face filled with concentration, Jack scanned the message that Artie had sent a couple of hours earlier.

"I tried to ring him too but he didn't answer," Fitch added, before slipping the phone carefully back in her pocket.

"And you've heard nothing else?" Jack rubbed his chin. "It does sound like a normal Artie wind-up, I must admit.

"But I would have thought he would have surfaced by now. And missing his tea is not usual at all."

Fitch allowed herself a small smile.

Someone else shared her concern – and Jack was someone she could trust.

Now they needed to find Artie.

19. SCHOOL

Fitch agreed to let go of Stanley's hand, much to the boy's delight.

The crowds were much thinner here as they moved away from the centre of the town's celebrations.

The boy happily skipped alongside her, loving every moment of the evening.

He was familiar with this small part of the town – his primary school was on the road ahead.

They had been busy bobbing into houses with lit-up pumpkins, picking up enough sweet treats to last for weeks.

Stanley's basket was nearly full. Fitch guessed she would be stuffing candy into her pockets before the night was out.

Fitch had left the primary school several years ago but she still knew the name of the street before the road sign even came into view: Givern Close.

"Fitch! Look over there!"

Stanley excitedly pointed towards a house situated

on the junction of the close. He jumped up and down with glee.

It had a tall hedge running around the edge of the garden.

Its gateway had been transformed into a gigantic dragon's mouth.

In the middle of the smoke-filled jaws, several bright red dragons were dishing out sweets to the large crowds of kids gathered around.

Stanley sounded giddy: "Can we go and queue up over there, please?"

Stanley grabbed Fitch's arm and began to drag her in the dragons' direction before she could protest.

They reached the back of the queue, which spilled into the road because of the huge number of people waiting.

It was the only really busy property in the neighbourhood unlike the homes near to the park, which were all packed.

Fitch scanned up and down the road. She could see the gates to Stanley's school from here.

Jack would be back in a moment.

He had disappeared earlier to tell his mates that he would be spending the rest of the evening with Fitch and Stanley.

They had agreed to meet outside the primary school and then they would begin to look for Artie together.

As the evening got later, families would slowly drift away for children's bedtimes and it would surely make it far easier to try to find their friend.

It wasn't the best plan that Fitch had ever heard but at least it was something.

Neither of them could come up with anything

better.

"Hey Stanley!"

"Hi Alvin."

A boy from Stanley's class walked past with his father. His basket was overflowing with goodies.

"Oooh, are you waiting for the deadly den of the dragons?

"They are so great. I wasn't scared at all."

His dad – a big burly man called Matt with grubby, paint-stained jeans – broke into a big smile.

"Of course, Alvin. You didn't hide behind me at all, did you?"

Alvin blushed.

"Well, it is really noisy and hot up there. But they are amazing.

"I liked the orange one the best. And they give you these awesome red fizzy worm things!"

He dangled one of the long and delicious-looking sweets in the air. Stanley's eyes bulged with eager anticipation.

"Wow!"

"Come on, Alvin. Time to go," said his dad, who began to move away. "Bye Stanley, have fun!"

Alvin hurriedly shoved the worm sweet back into his packed basket.

He spoke in a rush as his father led him down the street to the next house.

He shouted: "Don't forget to go over there!

"There is a really nice zombie mummy giving away whole chocolate bars! Bye Stan, see you tomorrow at school!"

Fitch and Stanley followed the direction where Alvin was pointing.

It was a dark-looking detached house. A massive

pumpkin sat on the doorstep next to the purple front door.

When Stanley turned back to say goodbye to his friend, Alvin and his father had already gone, lost in the crowds.

"Fitch, can I go and get a chocolate bar please? I'll ask for one for you too!"

Stanley was jiggling around in the queue with excitement.

Fitch shook her head.

"No, Stan. You know the rules, we stay together tonight."

Stanley grabbed her hand.

"Pleeeeeeaassssssseeeee Finny! That house is only over there!

"You can watch me all the way – and keep our place in this queue at the same time. It will take ages in this line."

Fitch hesitated.

He was right. It would take a while to get the front of this queue. There were at least 30 people ahead of them.

Stanley added: "And look, there's hardly anyone over there.

"I won't have to queue and I will be back in a minute easily. I am a fast runner. I do come here every single day for school, after all."

Fitch looked at his beaming face. The house was only 50 metres or so away and she could see the front door clearly too.

She bent down and looked sternly at Stanley.

"OK. Go there and come straight back! I'll be watching from here. Don't talk to any strangers. Be polite and make sure you say 'thank you'. Got it?"

Stanley nodded eagerly, obviously desperate to get his hands on the chocolate bars that Alvin had spoken of.

He set off across the road, weaving in and out of people towards the house on the far side of the junction.

Fitch shouted as Stanley moved further away.

"Stan?"

The little boy turned around and looked back at her nervously, thinking that she was going to stop him.

Instead she smiled.

"Don't you dare call me Finny again."

Stanley gave a double thumbs up. He turned and began to race towards the house with the giant pumpkin.

20. GONE

Fitch watched as Stanley happily trotted across the road in the direction of the dark house on the junction. The youngster was right: he could run quickly – and wasted no time.

Families walked along the road between them, laughing and joking in their fancy dress outfits.

It was not a problem – there were not enough bodies to block her view of the boy for more than a fleeting moment.

But Artie's disappearance was beginning to make Fitch worry.

The joke, it appeared, had worn thin.

Alarm bells had properly started to ring when Jack convinced her that he didn't know anything about Artie's no-show.

Artie Eason was an experienced practical joker.

He never allowed a stunt to overrun – because that would ruin the impact of the prank. Timing was everything and Artie knew that.

Yet this whole situation had gone on for too long to be amusing anymore.

And that was what worried her.

Stanley had reached the path to the house, passing a happy family-of-three who were busy stuffing chocolate bars into a carrier bag.

They let Stanley past on the narrow garden path and were soon lost in the crowd heading towards their next trick-or-treat destination.

Fitch realised she was gripping her hands together tightly. Her nails had dug deep into her skin, leaving blood-red marks on her palms.

Worries over Artie being possibly missing were understandable, but she was unsure why she was so uptight as she watched Stanley.

It was Halloween after all.

Children were supposed to knock on people's doors and ask for chocolates.

But the nagging feeling in her stomach would not go away.

There was something wrong. Somewhere close.

It was not Artie. It was something else but Fitch could not put her finger on it.

"Excuse me!"

Fitch snapped out of her daydream and turned to look at the man behind her, who was busy jabbing his finger over her shoulder.

She turned back toward the people in front of her – and immediately understood what he meant.

While she had been daydreaming, the queue she had been standing in had moved forward.

"Sorry!" She mumbled her apologies towards the people behind and took several steps forward to close up the gap again.

Fitch settled again and looked for Stanley.

The boy had reached the door and was standing on tiptoes to reach the doorbell.

With a stretch, he managed to push the buzzer. Chuffed with himself, he turned and gave Fitch a thumbs-up with the biggest smile to match.

Fitch waved back.

Then she felt a buzz in her pocket.

Her heart leapt.

Artie.

She pulled the smartphone out in a flash.

It was him.

She did not wait for him to speak.

"Artie! Where are you! I've been so worried. Are you OK?"

Fitch's words tumbled out in a rush.

There was a pause and then a loud crackle.

Silence.

"Artie? Can you hear me?"

The reply did come but only the odd word could be understood.

Wherever Artie was, his phone signal was poor but there could be no doubt that it was his voice.

For a second, she thought she might cry. Her best friend was OK.

But something was definitely wrong. The way that Artie spoke was not normal. He sounded scared.

The words were broken up, jumbled and did not come over as full sentences.

"Yes … did you … danger … bright light … shine … eyes … pumpkins … don't go … Flamingo … Givern.…"

Fitch could feel her heart pounding again as she tried to work out what her friend was saying.

She froze. Did he say Givern? They were on Givern Close.

Fitch pressed the phone closer to her ear and

spoke loudly: "Artie? What do you mean?

"What on earth is going on? Where are you? Are you OK?"

The phone signal gave up.

The call ended.

Artie was gone.

She glared at the phone screen and pounded the redial button.

"Come on, come on," Fitch muttered to herself.

She should have listened to her gut feeling from the beginning.

Dread seeped through her body. Now she knew: something was wrong.

It was no surprise when the call went straight to through to Artie's answerphone.

A hand reached out of nowhere and grabbed her arm.

Fitch yelped with fright and dropped the phone.

It bounced off the kerb and shattered into hundreds of pieces on the concrete floor.

"Woah!"

Fitch twisted around to see a wary looking Jack take a step away from her.

Both of his hands were held out in front of him to show he had not meant for that to happen.

Fitch looked at her friend. The phone did not matter. She could feel the tears begin to fall on to her face as she spoke.

"Oh Jack. It's Artie. He just rang but I couldn't understand what he was trying to say.

"Something is wrong, Jack, it is really wrong – and I don't know what to do."

Before she knew it, he stepped forward and hugged her – ignoring the remains of her now useless phone on the ground.

Jack hugged his friend tightly as she continued to sob into his shoulder.

He tried to soothe her: "Don't worry Fitch, everything is going to be all right.

"We will find him, I promise you. Artie Eason would not give up on us and we won't let him down either.

"Now dry those tears, Fitch. We need you. I need you."

Fitch smiled, although her body was still shaking.

She moved away and wiped her eyes.

"Thank you. He said a load of stuff but the phone reception was terrible and I didn't understand most of it.

"It was the way he spoke though – I knew it was serious.

"He definitely said something about 'danger' and 'Givern Close'. I am sure of that."

Jack raised his eyebrows.

"Wow. OK, let's take his advice and get away from here. Where's Stanley?"

Fitch's eyes widened.

Stanley.

She had forgotten about him.

"He is over…."

Jack followed her fingers as Fitch pointed in the direction of the dark house across the road.

The porch was empty.

21. MISSING

Fitch screamed.

It was a sound that started in her toes and rushed through her entire body, turning into a roar of despair as it left her mouth.

She forgot everything else.

Halloween. Jack. The queue. The dragons. Her broken phone. Artie.

None of that mattered now.

Everything had changed.

Seconds earlier she had watched Stanley cross the road towards the house with the giant pumpkin.

Now there was no-one.

In a flash she had dropped the basket of sweets and was running towards the house.

In the distant background, Fitch could hear Jack calling out to her but she did not respond.

Chocolate and packets of sweets fell from her full pockets, scattering across the concrete as the girl dodged past shocked onlookers.

Panic rose up into her throat.

"He's fine. He's fine. He's got to be fine."

She hoped Stanley would miraculously appear but there was still no-one in front of the house.

Perhaps he was waiting inside?

If he had gone into the house to grab sweets, Stanley would be in big trouble.

The younger boy knew only too well that he had to stay where she could see him.

Fitch dashed up the neatly trimmed garden path to the house. The closer she got to the property, the more sinister it seemed.

And not in a Halloween-themed way either.

It was dark outside yet the house had no lights on inside either. It was odd – like there was no-one living there.

Fitch only slowed down when she reached the exact spot where Stanley had turned and cheerfully waved to her.

Now it was just her.

She rang the doorbell and waited.

No light came on.

The front door remained closed.

Fitch was panting for breath.

It was not the running that had caused the breathlessness – she was as fit as a fiddle and could run for miles – but the panic that was spreading through her body.

She fought to control it, making herself take deep breaths.

She knocked this time, rapping the sturdy door hard enough to make her knuckles throb with pain.

No answer again.

She cupped both hands against the frosted glass window pane within the dark purple door and peered into the gloom.

The hallway was unlit and blurry – but no shadows moved and there were no young boys waiting patiently for sweets.

"Stanley!" Fitch screamed in desperate hope. A few heads turned in concern but there was still no sign of him.

"Fitch?"

She turned, knowing it was Jack who was standing close by.

"Stanley is in here. He must be. He wouldn't just run off – he's a good boy."

Jack came closer and gently put an arm around her shoulder.

"I know, I know," he said soothingly. "He could be anywhere though, Fitch, couldn't he?"

Fitch stared at Jack and then back at the house.

"No. He is definitely in there. He has to be.

"I saw him press the doorbell only a few seconds ago. He was here."

Jack looked around, doubt spread across his tanned face.

Fitch continued: "It was the call from Artie. That distracted me. I...."

Artie.

Her mind flashed back to the broken phone conversation they had earlier.

"Oh no. Artie tried to tell me. I remember he clearly said 'Givern' when he rang. It was hard to make out the words but I know what I heard.

"This house is on Givern Close. I know that this was the place he was trying to warn us about. He was just too late."

Tears were beginning to well up in her eyes. Fitch

bit her lip.

Crying would not help anyone, she reminded herself harshly.

She continued: "Stan would not have gone anywhere else without me. His friend Alvin told him to come here.

"Alvin and his dad told us that the house with the giant pumpkin had a mummy handing out whole chocolate bars.

"It was this one right here."

Fitch's stomach lurched at the thought of Stanley being alone and frightened without her.

She rapped hard on the solid front door again but stopped when she saw the puzzled look on Jack's face.

"Jack? What are you looking at? What is it? What's wrong?"

His eyes darted around the ground.

She tried to follow his gaze but could not see anything out of the ordinary.

"Jack!"

She shouted despite standing next to him.

He looked at her with a strange expression on his face.

Jack spoke softly: "You need to stop knocking on the door and ringing the bell. We need to leave."

Fitch raised her eyebrows. Had he gone mad?

Jack grimaced: "There's no pumpkin here, Fitch.

"I'm sorry but this place isn't even part of the Pumpkin Code."

22. SEARCHING

The pumpkin was here. I know it was, Fitch thought to herself, as her eyes fell to the floor.

But Jack was right: there was no pumpkin outside the house.

The girl began to twist and turn looking around for the giant lantern that she was certain had been perched on the porch.

She remembered clearly: it had been so big that both her and Stanley could see it from the queue across the road.

But it wasn't here now. Had she imagined it?

Fitch did not know but, in truth, she did not care. Either way, Stanley was inside the house, she was sure of it.

"Artie warned us. I know that Stanley's in there," Fitch replied through gritted teeth. "I'm going to look around the back. He must be here."

The tears began to fall freely from her cheeks. She did not try to fight them or brush them away.

Jack held up his hands. He did not want to start an

argument. It would not help anyone.

Jack spoke softly and slowly, like he was choosing his words with painstaking care: "OK. You check out the back garden. I'll do a quick lap down by the school and the nearby streets.

"Maybe Stanley's managed to get lost somehow. Or perhaps someone has seen him and can point us in the right direction?

"We need to check all of the possibilities, don't we?"

Fitch waved a hand in his direction. She knew Jack was trying to help but she was barely listening to his words.

She nodded towards the house: "You do what you like. He's in here."

Fitch turned away from her friend without another word and followed the deep red brickwork of the house towards the large wooden fence.

A pair of green and brown wheelie bins provided the perfect step for her to vault the barrier, which she did with ease.

And then she was gone.

Jack stood and watched as his friend disappeared out of sight without a backwards glance.

For a second, he thought about going over the fence with her – but they needed to split up.

It was quite obvious that there was no-one in the house but Fitch would not listen to reason at the moment.

Stanley could easily have wandered off into the town and lost his bearings.

They needed to be calm and check every possibility – rather than plunge straight into the wild goose chase that Fitch seemed determined to get involved in.

Jack twisted away from the house and began to move at top speed. In a matter of seconds, he'd left the garden behind and ran along the street towards the primary school.

"Stanley! Stanley!"

Jack's voice rang out over the din of the spooky celebrations.

No response.

And no-one else appeared interested either.

There was too much happening elsewhere.

Jack reached the primary school gates. They were locked with a hefty padlock. The cul-de-sac ended with the school's entrance.

Unless Stanley was hiding in one of the gardens, he wasn't here.

A brief kick of the iron gates confirmed they were sealed shut and there was no way of getting through.

That was enough for Jack.

He quickly doubled back and soon found himself back at the junction with the house where Fitch had bunked over the fence.

For a moment, he considered again going to find his friend and stopping her from breaking the trespass law.

But Stanley needed him.

In his mind, he pictured the little boy all alone crying among the hordes of dressed-up monsters and ghouls.

Halloween could be scary even for those who knew it was all in fun. For someone who was Stanley's age, it must be terrifying.

Jack could feel his palms becoming sweaty with anxiety.

He turned his back on the detached house and began to move towards the centre of the celebrations – in the direction of where he had first bumped into Stanley and Fitch earlier that evening.

His long legs weaved at pace through the groups of people – some of whom he recognised and others he did not.

All the time he was scanning the streets for a little figure of Shrek on his own.

Then, just as he was hitting full flow, a deep voice called out to him.

"Jack?"

The teenager turned around in a flash and saw Alvin's dad Matt standing a couple of feet away.

Jack screeched to a halt: "Err, hi there! Have you seen Stanley?"

Matt rubbed his chin, which was covered in white make-up, as he considered the question.

"No. We haven't seen him since we saw him and Fitch over by the dragons."

Jack was already walking away.

They were no help.

"Thanks – gotta go!"

Then Alvin appeared out of nowhere, still proudly clutching the wiggly worm sweet that he had shown Stanley earlier.

"He was going to the house with the giant pumpkin!"

Jack stopped in his tracks and turned back to face the little boy.

He bent down so he could hear the boy clearly amid all the noise: "What?"

Alvin grinned.

"Yes, we told him to go to the house on the

corner! There was a mummy with blood squirted everywhere and she was giving out proper chocolate bars to everyone. It was the best...."

Alvin did not get the chance to finish his sentence.

Jack's mouth had fallen open as Alvin revealed the truth.

He did not say goodbye.

He simply turned and ran – knocking people flying as he charged back towards the darkened house.

Fitch had been right all along yet he had chosen not to listen.

Now she was heading into terrible trouble.

And she was all alone.

23. UNCOVERED

Like a cat, Fitch landed without a sound on the other side of the fence.

She looked behind her, half hoping that Jack would change his mind and follow her tracks.

But the fence remained still.

She was alone.

Fitch returned her gaze to the garden in front of her. An old shed stood to her left and the wall of the house to her right.

A cracked concrete path separated the two and lay directly in front of her.

She pushed herself against the wall to stop her shadow spilling into the garden and provide an early warning to anyone lurking in the house.

Fitch did not know why she was so scared. But a combination of Artie's muffled warning and something deep inside told her to be careful.

Too much had happened tonight that made no sense.

Evil was in the air.

She could somehow feel it.

Fitch reached the end of the wall and peeked around the corner into the square rear garden.

Another large shed that looked like a small house stood at the far end of the garden.

"Wow, who are these people?" Fitch thought to herself.

She did not know anyone else who had two garden sheds.

The large one in front of her looked similar to an expensive log cabin.

Between the house and the expensive shed stood a neatly kept lawn surrounded by bushes and shrubs.

The back door stood to her right.

She noted the powerful security light hovering over the main door, which pointed towards the lawn.

Fitch guessed she could scoot under the light's sensors if she edged along the wall carefully.

She turned the corner and, taking care to duck under a small ground floor window, she crept along the brickwork.

Fitch reached the white plastic of the door moments later. A quick peek through the thick window pane revealed an empty, modern-looking kitchen.

She returned to her crouched position and considered the options.

There were two choices for her: either go into the kitchen or keep walking along the wall to the double patio doors at the far end of the house.

A dim ray of light spilled out from the double doors – telling Fitch that she needed to choose the kitchen if she wanted the element of surprise. It was the first sign of life she'd seen coming from the house. Fitch's eyes narrowed – she knew there was somebody in there. Why would they hide and not answer the door?

She picked up a rock off the floor that was the size of a baseball.

She would have to smash one of the windows if the doors were locked.

Deep in the back of her mind, Fitch knew she would get into big trouble for this.

It was completely wrong.

Her dad would go crazy when he found out that she was breaking the law.

She had never done anything like this before.

But she knew Stanley was in there.

She could not explain exactly how she knew but something in her gut told her that he was in trouble.

Big trouble.

The thought of Stanley spurred her on. With a deep breath, Fitch carefully turned the handle of the door.

Nothing.

It did not budge an inch.

It was a new door – it needed more force. With a small grunt, she tugged the handle downwards.

To her relief, the lock popped into action. She heard the mechanism grind and then it opened in front of her.

Fitch was in.

Clutching the rock close to her chest, she stepped into the house.

Blood pounded through her veins.

She was convinced that other people would be able to hear her heartbeat as it throbbed inside her chest.

Fitch shook her head to clear her thoughts.

Time was essential. She could not waste a single second.

Leaving the door open in case she had to make a quick exit, Fitch moved across the kitchen in speedy silence.

As she already knew, it was empty and she moved to the doorway in the heart of the house.

She reached for the handle and realised her hands were trembling.

Fitch ignored the feeling of fear building up inside her body and forced it back down inside her.

The door was slightly ajar so the merest push opened up the hallway in front of her.

Fitch moved into the hallway with the rock held up high, ready to strike.

She froze. There it was.

The giant pumpkin that had enticed people to the house now sat in the hallway.

Its candle had been extinguished – it was no wonder that her and Jack had missed it when they peered through the glass panes on the porch.

She had been right.

But it proved something else too: this had been a trap.

24. RESCUE

Fitch stared at the unnaturally large pumpkin at her feet.

It was the biggest pumpkin she'd ever seen with a crazy expression carved into the side.

Several candles had been used to burn brightly inside the pumpkin.

Now they stood half-burned. It was unlikely they would ever be used again.

In the semi dark, it looked far creepier than any other pumpkin out there.

Fitch shivered.

She weighed up her options again. Discovering the pumpkin had brought her to a halt. She needed to refocus.

The porch door stood at the far end of the hallway with the stairs in the middle of the room.

It left Fitch with a choice of two wooden doors.

Both were closed.

One was directly opposite her. The other stood near the front door.

She remembered how the ray of light came from the patio windows – and instantly made up her mind.

In a couple of strides, she crossed the width of the hallway.

Fitch guessed it was either a large room on the other side of the door or two smaller rooms.

Either way, she was going in.

She tried to swallow but realised her throat was bone dry.

The rock weighed heavy in her hand.

Her ears strained to hear the tell-tale sounds of Stanley. She could hear faint murmurs of activity behind the door but could not place them.

Fitch paused.

Should she cautiously open the door?

Or should she fling it open and try to take advantage of her surprise?

Then she heard a loud noise. It was a clear and familiar sound.

Stanley.

She could not work out the words but it was definitely him.

And he was close.

Any thoughts of planning or caution went out of the window.

She forgot everything else. Her heart leapt.

Fitch snatched at the door handle and flung it open without a second thought.

The door opened without a fight.

Two strides later, she found herself in the centre of a modern living room.

It was a strange, dimly lit room. There was hardly any furniture and no pictures or paintings on the walls.

However, she did not care.

Right in front of her stood Stanley Eason.

The small boy had his back to her and was about to delve into a leather bag with a strange yellow glow oozing from it.

The odd light – the same one that Fitch had seen from outside – did not look natural.

"Stan! What on earth…."

The boy span round in shock exactly as Fitch dived towards him.

She crashed into him at speed and the impact of the collision was enough to send the bag flying into the wall before it dropped to the floor.

Seconds later, the brown bag's strange light disappeared and the room went dark.

"Owwwww!"

Fitch and Stanley lay on the floor together, their legs and arms tangled up with each other.

She hugged him tightly, not wanting to let him go. It was only then did she realise he was trying to say something.

Then she heard an awful wail from behind the door.

"No! It is not possible. Drat you!"

The female voice hissed throughout the room but Fitch could not see who it belonged to.

She guessed it was the mummy character that Alvin had mentioned earlier.

It was high-pitched and reminded Fitch of the awful sound when someone rang their fingernails down a blackboard.

"Stanley had said that his big friend would be worried about him and would soon come looking for him.

"And he was right!

"Here you are, my dear, trying to ruin everything with your pathetic rescue act.

"I am sick to death of kids in this town sticking their noses in and trying to interfere in our business."

With a grunt, Fitch pushed Stanley off her as she heard the woman begin to move towards them.

The rock – her only weapon – had been dropped as she had dived to protect Stanley from the glowing bag. It was near the door and could not help now.

Fitch got to her feet stood to face the woman, holding her hands out in front of her.

"Look missus. I have no idea who you are and I don't care.

"I am sure this is a mistake. All round. Let's forget it and move on, shall we?"

The woman approached Fitch quicker than humanly possible.

Instantly Fitch knew this woman would not listen to reason.

She replied with a sickly sweet grin fixed on her face: "Forget it? Move on? Oh no, that doesn't work for me at all, my dear."

Stanley remained in a tangle on the floor so Fitch stepped across him to make sure he was behind her. The closer the woman got, the more insane she looked.

Fitch steeled herself. And then everything went black.

25. THE TRAIL

Jack vaulted the fence with ease.

He had never run so fast in his life.

Shouting at the top of his voice to watch out, people either moved out of the way or got bowled over.

He flew through the sea of people without barely breaking stride.

Soon he reached the detached house. It looked no different to the last time he was here.

He had been wrong then. He should have believed Fitch the first time around.

Now he hoped it was not too late.

A quick test of the front door handle had revealed what he already knew: it was locked and he needed to follow in Fitch's footsteps.

Jack did not waste time trying to keep quiet.

He could not see Fitch and he guessed it was a bad sign.

The back door was slightly ajar. He ghosted into the kitchen, ears pricked to try to detect the merest sound.

Nothing.

He reached the doorway into the hallway.

That door was open too.

Fitch had come this way before him.

He saw the giant pumpkin in the hall. Beads of sweat began to trickle down his back as he realised she had been right.

Jack did not linger. He went straight into the room opposite.

It had been trashed. Stanley's basket of treats were strewn over the floor.

Jack gasped.

Small drops of red were splattered over the cream carpet.

Blood.

Jack dropped to his knees and lightly touched the liquid.

It was still wet.

There was a cluster of droplets near the fake fireplace but only the odd drop here and there after that.

The faint trail led towards the door leading to the stairs.

And the freshness of the blood told him they must still be close.

He stood up and backtracked to the hallway, which was still empty. The downstairs toilet was also deserted.

That only left him one option – to go up to the next floor.

Jack climbed the stairs three at a time and found himself on a large landing.

Five doors stood in front of him. They were all

closed.

"Fitch! Stanley!"

He yelled loudly, hoping to pick up some clue – a muffled reply, a rustle of movement, a scream – anything would do.

No response came.

He paused for a moment, desperately hoping for an answer.

Nothing still.

Jack could not wait any longer.

He barged into the room on his right and found himself in an empty study.

The small bedroom was the same, and there was nobody in the medium-sized bedroom.

The newly decorated marble bathroom was deserted too.

Jack felt goose bumps on his skin.

The house did not feel like a home. Everything was perfect, not a single thing was out of place.

But there were no possessions. No televisions. Or trainers. Or bottles of shampoo. Or rubbish. There was nothing.

It was odd.

He steeled himself as he faced the last door.

With a loud creak, the master bedroom opened up before him.

In desperation, Jack rushed past the king-sized bed and kicked open the en suite door.

Empty.

They were not here.

He was too late.

"No!"

Jack slammed his fists down on the toilet's window sill in anger.

He had let them down.

Fitch.

Stanley.

He was supposed to keep them safe.

And he had failed.

They had been here – and not long ago either.

Where had they gone?

What was he missing?

Could they not hear his shouting?

Jack's phone buzzed in his pocket, making him jump.

The screen revealed the caller's name: Artie.

"Artie. Hello. I'm so sorry … sorry … they've gone.

"I don't know how it … Stanley … I tried … Fitch … I should have.…"

Jack paused.

He knew he wasn't making much sense.

But he quickly realised Artie could not hear him properly.

He stopped talking and tried to listen to the broken sentences coming from his friend, his face screwed up in concentration.

"Goblins? Fancy dress? Light in whose eyes? What do you mean, mate?"

Artie did not reply. His words were coming across in chunks and not making much sense to Jack.

The phone went dead.

Jack hit redial but the call ended instantly.

No signal.

How could that possibly be?

They were just talking a few seconds ago.

He tried again. No signal.

Jack felt an unnatural heat inside his chest as panic

spread.

He had not even managed to properly tell his friend about Stanley and Fitch going missing.

And Artie had not been listening anyway.

Goblins?

What on earth had happened to him tonight?

Jack knew he could not worry about Artie at the moment. At least he was OK.

His complete attention needed to focus on Fitch and Stanley.

In desperate need of inspiration, he wandered back into the bedroom and opened the window blind. He found himself overlooking the back garden as he weighed up his next move.

At the far end of the yard stood a large wooden shed with large windows. Inside, a light shone brightly.

With a snap of his fingers, he realised the terrible truth: he had been looking for his friends in the wrong building.

PART THREE

UNDERGROUND

26. RUNAWAY

The mobile phone soared into the air before quickly falling and nestling deep in the roots of a dark-looking shrub.

A dull crack suggested the lightweight handset had been smashed.

Light from the screen flickered for a moment – enough to provide an idea of its location – before petering out.

Artie spun around, furious that he had let the goblin outwit him.

Berry had seemed so weak, almost as if life was leaving him as every minute passed.

Now he was somehow standing with a fearsome look plastered on his face as he approached Artie for a second time.

He held a large wooden club, the weapon he had used to knock the phone clean out of Artie's hands moments earlier.

He sneered: "Well, well, well. Look who's in

trouble now."

Without the phone, the teenager was defenceless.

A fact the goblin knew only too well.

With a wheezy breath, Berry swung the heavy tree branch.

The wild blow missed but forced Artie to jump out of the way.

His right trainer lost grip in the mud and Artie's back leg slipped, forcing him to drop to his knees in the darkness.

Berry's wheezing was close but the goblin was hidden by the long shadows.

Artie tensed as he braced for the attack.

He waited in the gloom.

Nothing happened.

The sounds of heavy breathing disappeared. Only the whispers of moving leaves could be heard.

Berry had gone.

"He's making a run for it," Artie realised with a jolt. "That sneaky devil!"

The boy climbed to his feet and brushed the mud off his knees. Then he remembered his phone: the only weapon he had.

He halted. He would have to let Berry go. His phone was too important.

As his hands searched the damp earth and jagged-edged thorns, Artie's mind replayed the last few minutes.

The phone call had been a bad decision.

His attempt to warn his friends about the goblins' plan – and tell them about their enemies' weakness for light – had been nothing short of a disaster.

Finding any kind of reception had been difficult enough. Fitch answered his call the first time around but the line went dead after about 10 seconds. He was unsure how much she had heard.

When he tried to ring back, there had been no reception available. It had taken him ages to find a single bar of reception and, when he tried to ring her for a second time, he got no answer.

In panic, he had rung Jack, who, to Artie's relief, answered.

He could not hear anything his friend said, so he relayed the story – as much as he knew, at least – and hoped Jack could understand. He had tried to warn his friends and, crucially, tell them about the goblins' weakness that could save their lives. Hopefully it would be enough. He could not do any more at the moment.

The top of his fingers grazed over the phone's case. It was the faintest touch but enough for Artie to know its whereabouts.

Within seconds, the phone was out of the bush and back in his hand.

Artie pushed down the power button and the badly damaged screen – much to his relief – flashed into life.

With the fresh cracks running down the display, the phone reverted back to the phone's call log.

The call to Jack had lasted for 23 seconds before Berry knocked it out of his hands.

Despite running low on battery, the phone was still working. It was the only weapon he had and he had to protect it.

Kids' lives may depend on it.

Maybe Stanley's.

Possibly Fitch's.

Even Jack's.

Definitely his own.

Artie gritted his teeth. He would not let that happen.

He tucked the phone back into his pocket and his thoughts returned to the task of finding Berry.

The goblin was badly hurt. His breathing had been struggling with strange spots of green dripping from his face.

Light from the phone had caused serious damage to him.

When Artie had accidentally thrust his mobile in the goblin's face, the injury had been severe.

Berry had clutched his face in agony.

He moaned and writhed in pain as Artie had questioned him.

In the main, the goblin had refused to answer the questions – despite being severely injured.

But the monster still hadn't been able to resist the odd gloat or two.

"You're in big trouble, boy," he wheezed as Artie had stood over him. "You think you've won but you know nothing."

Artie's cheeks had instantly flushed with anger and he grabbed the front of Berry's torn shirt.

"Perhaps not, but I got you, didn't I?"

Berry let out a raspy chuckle and pushed the hand away. "Luck! Pure luck and nothing else," he spat at his enemy.

"You got Birch by accidentally setting off that security light. Once they rushed to save him, I knew it was only me who could catch you…."

Berry cast an evil look in Artie's direction.

"Of course, I had also forgotten my glasses but I didn't realise you would understand our weakness so quickly."

He stopped talking abruptly, looking into the distance with a strange look upon his face.

Artie leaned in closer: "The light? That's your weakness? Is that why you all wear sunglasses? How does it work?"

Berry blinked and his attention returned to the boy in front of him.

He sneered: "We are so much stronger, quicker and cleverer than humans.

"Our bodies have adapted over time.

"Yet one thing from our long-gone cave-dwelling days remains – our eyes cannot cope with bright light.

"I don't mean normal light, of course. Just bright, intense light close to our eyeballs.

"If we have our sunglasses, then it is no problem, but if we forget them...."

The goblin tailed off again.

And, much to Artie's annoyance, he had refused to say anything more.

But it had been his actions that had given him away.

As the questions continued, Berry made repeated attempts to crawl away.

Artie had been curious: where was he going?

The teenager kept talking while watching the creature crawl painfully towards its unknown goal.

As he watched the goblin inching slowly away, Artie had decided to ring his friends.

He did not believe Berry would be a threat.

Yet he had been mistaken.

Badly wrong.

First, the goblin had cackled wickedly as Artie's call to Fitch cut out.

"You fool!

"Ridgeon had thought of that!

"There's no mobile phones around here tonight that will work! We have seen to that."

Artie had turned his back on the taunts but the words struck a chord with him – his conversation with Fitch had been a disaster.

The gloating goblin had been right: to Artie's intense frustration, the same thing happened when he rang Jack.

As the call ended, he had come mightily close to being clobbered by the goblin.

Where Berry had summoned the strength to attack him, Artie did not know.

But he had almost destroyed Artie's phone.

Then he was gone.

Artie grimaced and shook his head.

He had no choice – he had to follow Berry into the deeper part of the woods.

And he needed to find him quick.

27. GOING UNDER

Being stealthy was no longer required.

Jack bounded down the stairs three at a time and raced to the living room where the splatters of blood still coated the cream carpet. He flicked on the light and studied the room carefully.

It made sense now.

The trail of blood did not lead upstairs. It had been a devious fake – one created to throw others off the scent.

Very clever, Jack conceded.

Instead, whoever had captured Fitch and Stanley had moved them into the large shed at the bottom of the garden.

Jack dragged open the curtains and yanked the patio doors apart. It slid back immediately – it had been unlocked.

The boy shook his head.

He must have missed them by seconds. Perhaps they had even snuck out of the house while he was inside.

Fear ran through his body.

He knew there was no way that Fitch would go quietly.

Why hadn't she shouted to him?

Was she hurt?

The blood in the house was fresh. Instinct told him that it was his friend's.

"Concentrate. They need you," he reminded himself. He could not start panicking – that would not help anybody.

Light from the house poured out on to the lawn. Jack silently covered the small patch of grass in a matter of seconds.

He pushed up against the wooden wall of the fancy shed. Jack was tall so could no longer hide easily but the shadows helped to cover most of him.

The building was not a normal shed. It did not house lawnmowers and rusty garden equipment.

This was more like an expensive log cabin. It had electricity, huge windows and heating.

Risking a look through the window, Jack could see a large flat screen TV, a fancy coffee machine and one of the latest games consoles with a VR headset.

There was no-one inside the room.

With his heart pounding, Jack tried the door handle. It was unlocked.

The door screeched a little as he opened it wide enough to slip through.

Jack paused.

The sound had been loud enough to let them know that someone was coming in.

But no-one came to investigate.

Everything remained still and quiet.

The only noise came from the distant cries and

screams of people still enjoying Halloween.

The normal world was a stone's throw away but it seemed like a different planet to Jack.

Satisfied no-one was coming to investigate, he left the door open and squatted behind the leather couch in front of the games console.

At least the open door would provide an easy escape route for him.

Spots of fresh blood on the floor caught his eye.

This time they led to the door embedded in the wall opposite him.

Jack did not hesitate. Either Fitch or Stanley were bleeding so every second mattered.

And he had wasted far too much time already.

He burst through the door with his fists raised.

Again, it was empty.

But it was quite obvious they had been there.

A heavy-looking trapdoor had been left wide open in the middle of the room.

There was nothing else in the room apart from a red toolbox, which stood opened in the corner. It looked brand new.

The upper part of the toolbox was empty.

Half-heartedly, Jack lifted up the tray to discover a sharp-looking hatchet sitting along with a handful of nuts and bolts in the base of the box.

Jack had never used a small axe before but he picked it up and slotted it inside his jeans – like he had seen in the movies. It was better than nothing, he guessed.

He closed the toolbox up, crouched down and inspected the trapdoor.

A ladder was connected to the old damp brickwork heading downwards. A faint light displayed the bottom of the shaft.

It was a long way down.

Jack looked around for any other clues. There were none.

He had one choice – to follow them.

A small voice inside his head piped up: "This is a trap. It is so blatant. You know it. They know you're coming.

"They've even left a light on for you!"

Jack shook his head but pulled out his phone as he did so.

His fingers typed out a brief message to Artie – in the hope that his best friend's phone was back up and running.

He did not have time to call so the message would have to do.

He did not even know where Artie was or whether he would even see it – but it was the best he could do right now.

Jack shoved the phone back into his pocket and ditched the skeleton mask that dangled around his neck. He did not need it anymore.

The teenager swung his legs into the shaft, quickly finding the rungs of the iron ladder without even looking.

Within seconds he was fully inside the tunnel. A low rumbling came from deep within the underground lair.

Trap or not, he had to try.

He knew that he was Fitch and Stanley's only chance.

28. SURVIVAL

Fitch slowly opened an eye.

Immediately, her head throbbed with intense pain.

Trying to ignore the stinging pain, she tried to look around.

Where was she? It did not look anywhere familiar.

It was cold and smelt funny.

Her other eye would not open because something sticky kept it firmly closed.

Blood. Even the eye that was open could not focus properly. Every detail of her current surroundings was a blur.

She was lying down. Yet when Fitch tried to sit up, she realised both her wrists and feet had been tied together.

Her pulse quickened. How long had she been out for?

Other senses came alive.

Water was definitely flowing somewhere inside the tunnel.

The overpowering smell of damp refused to leave her nostrils. She could hear a continual trickle that –

Fitch guessed – was somewhere on the floor.

Slowly her vision began to improve and the pain became more of a dull ache. She peered closely at her surroundings.

Someone was lying next to her: Stanley.

The boy was facing the opposite direction but was also tied with reams of thick silver tape.

Fitch nudged him in the back with her knee.

No response.

She tried to speak his name but only a small croak emerged.

Nothing. In desperation, she booted Stanley with all her might and the boy flinched.

Fitch breathed a sigh of relief.

He was OK – probably too scared to move.

She croaked: "Don't worry Stan. It's going to be all right."

His head nodded a fraction in response. Stanley could hear her: he was alive and well.

Now she had to somehow untangle them both from this almighty mess.

As the minutes passed by her vision began to fully return. Fitch blinked furiously to try to get her normal eyesight back.

Finally, the blurry shapes began to turn clear.

They had been dumped in some type of trailer, the type that people used when they went on holiday with stacks of gear for several weeks.

There was nothing else in the trailer except her and Stanley.

Despite the relatively light load, they were still moving slowly.

Craning her neck, Fitch could still not see any vehicle ahead of them. She had no idea how they were being pulled.

Or were they being pushed?

No. A quick check revealed no-one behind them. She checked the rest of her surroundings.

They were in the middle of a long tunnel made from ancient bricks.

Huge intricate cobwebs laced large swathes of the curved ceiling above their heads.

Fitch shivered.

She hated spiders at the best of times.

She did not want to imagine how many lived down here in the darkness – until they had been rudely interrupted this evening.

Lights had been hung haphazardly along one of the tunnel's walls so everything was cast in a strange yellow glow.

Underneath the lights, a thick rope had been tied along the length of the tunnel wall.

Fitch could not guess why it was there but she did not care either.

Escape. That was the only thing mattered.

She studied the tape that had been wrapped tightly around her wrists.

Her ankles were pinned together too, although the bond felt slightly looser.

She began to wiggle her feet back and forth in a vain attempt to free herself. Spying a sharp lip on rear of the trailer, she gently guided the tape against the edge and began to grind her hips to put pressure on the tape.

Incredibly, it began to work. Within a minute or so, the tape was becoming frayed.

A cackle of static made Fitch stop with a jolt.

"Gillian?"

A man's voice echoed loudly. It sounded as if it was coming from a walk-talkie or some sort of radio.

"Yes?"

Fitch tensed. She knew that voice. It was the woman who had hit her.

Her evil ghoulish face was the last thing that Fitch had seen before the darkness had taken her.

She was somewhere in front of the trailer but Fitch could not shift her body to look forwards.

"Time is tight. Are you near?"

Fitch held her breath.

"We are close, Ridgeon. About five minutes or so away. I have a … bonus too."

More static.

"Say again, Gillian. I missed that last part."

The woman spoke again. The words were slow and deliberate, spoken with a hint of ice that made Fitch shiver.

"We will be there soon, Ridgeon. Be ready."

It sounded like the man knew better than to argue.

"Roger that. See you soon."

The radio static fizzled out.

Silence filled the tunnel once more as the trailer remained rooted to the spot.

Fitch held her breath.

She heard Gillian's chuntering under her breath but was unable to understand the words.

Then her ears picked up something different.

It was faint, somewhere in the far distance, but the echo was clear.

"Fitch? Stanley? Where are you two?"

Her heart leapt with joy.

She knew that voice. They were not alone.

Jack was somewhere down here too.

29. EXIT PLAN

Teeth chattering with cold, Artie stood on a small ridge with his phone shining down on Berry.

The goblin was dead.

Yet his body was … melting into the ground in front of the boy's eyes.

The stench was overpowering as green liquid seeped from Berry's tattered clothes and began to ooze over the ground.

The teenager could feel his jeans sticking to him, soaked from the unexpected dip in the pond earlier in the evening.

It was freezing.

He would catch a chill, for sure.

But he stood transfixed, silently watching the strange gunge seep into the soil using his phone's flashlight.

Berry had been easy to track down once Artie had recovered his phone.

The goblin's struggle for air had given him away, the raspy breaths allowing Artie to find the runaway in a matter of minutes.

As Artie had closed in, Berry had smiled wickedly as he looked back at the approaching boy.

"You silly, silly boy," he'd said. "You can't beat us.

"We always survive.

"You know nothing."

With an evil cackle and a painful wheeze, Berry shuddered for a final time and became still.

Artie was alone.

For a moment, he considered trying to ring Jack or Fitch again but decided against it.

He still had no idea if Jack had understood the initial message or not, but he had to save his phone battery.

It was already down to 17 per cent and he sensed he would need every ounce of its power.

But he did not know what to do next.

Ever since he had stumbled across the goblins, he had been chased throughout a maze of paths, ponds, gardens and bushes.

He was finally free of them but something else was wrong and Artie could not quite place his finger on it.

He glanced to his right – the place where Berry had died.

The goblin was definitely gone. Artie was certain of that but the smell seemed to be getting more powerful all the time.

"Think Eason, think!"

Artie spoke aloud, aware there was no-one to hear his words.

He cocked his head to one side.

Where had Berry been going?

Artie wrinkled his nose, deep in thought.

The goblin had not been heading back towards the house, where Ridgeon and the others would surely be waiting.

Indeed, that house – and Artie's own back garden – had been left far behind.

Had he been trying to lead the enemy away from their base? Or did he have another escape route in mind?

Artie began to carefully inspect the area around him with new interest.

He stood in a thicker part of the wood, where there was less light and the bushes grew thick and spiky.

It was almost on the outskirts of town – the rumble from evening traffic using one of the town's main roads could be clearly heard.

The steep slope overlooked a dense mass of brambles and shrubs. To Artie's left, a muddy path went downwards.

Something told him that this group of goblins were too selfish to worry about protecting others. The others had abandoned Berry, after all.

Artie wasn't sure but he guessed Berry was trying to save himself – and had come here for a reason.

He moved slowly, looking around.

One wrong step and he could plummet down the slope and hurt himself badly.

And if he had a broken leg, he would be no use to anyone.

In a couple of minutes, he reached the base of the slope. It was pitch black here. He checked his phone again – 15 per cent battery now.

He switched to power-saving mode and turned off the flashlight.

The brightness from the large screen was not as powerful but it still provided enough light to see at short range.

However, he still could not see anything that may help – certainly not something that Berry may have been desperately aiming for.

Apart from a few planks of wood discarded against the brambles, there was no sign that anyone had been here for a long time.

The passing traffic sounded louder down here.

Artie turned his attention away from the bushes to gauge how far he was from the main road.

He took several steps towards the light, which came from the street lamps overlooking the road in the distance.

Within 20 metres or so, the bushes became thinner as the light penetrated the outer edges of the wood.

It made walking easier and Artie covered the ground quickly.

The shadows slowly disappeared as the light streamed in.

Apart from one.

The thick gloom had stopped Artie from seeing the dark shape in the thicket.

But, as he got closer, it was clear there was no light passing through it.

Artie reached out and touched the mysterious object.

It was a bulky tarpaulin cover, similar to one that his mother used to cover their barbecue with every winter.

Rain had made the waterproof material even heavier than usual and Artie could only lift it a fraction.

It was enough to tell him what he needed to know.

Two tyres could be clearly seen.

With a dull thud, Artie let the tarpaulin drop back into place.

His heart was racing.

Berry had been heading to the goblins' secret getaway car.

30. CLOSING IN

For decades, Foston had been a busy mining town.

The coal mine had long since closed and plush new offices had sprung up in its place.

And the old-fashioned railway, which served the town for more than a century, had been a museum for years.

Schoolchildren across the region were given the opportunity to visit the town's mine every summer.

Jack had visited when he was younger, perhaps aged 10 or so.

Yet this tunnel was nothing remotely like ones that the miners used.

Jack guessed it must be one of the old railway tunnels that still zigzagged underneath the town.

The brickwork felt sturdy and well-crafted – as if it could easily stand for another 100 years without too much trouble.

But the water puzzled him. It was barely raining.

Why was the floor so wet?

He pushed the thought to the back of his mind as he looked up and down the tunnel.

It was dimly lit in both directions.

He could hear a distant rumble of a vehicle but it

was impossible to know which direction it was coming from.

"Fitch? Stanley? Where are you two?"

He regretted shouting as soon as the words left his mouth.

If the kidnappers did not know they were being followed, they did now.

There was no answer either.

Jack looked left and right as the voice in his mind urged him to hurry up.

Finally, he chose to head left.

The lights looked a little brighter that way, he told himself. Really, it was nothing but a guess.

He let go of the bottom rung of the ladder, which came up to his shoulder. The shaft upwards was dark – it could easily be missed.

He ditched the black Halloween outfit in a pile on the floor. It was not needed and it would only slow him down. Underneath Jack wore jeans and a red T-shirt that his mum had bought for him last week. He hoped she would understand what he had to do next.

Jack carefully scooped the hatchet out of his jeans.

Its razor-sharp blade tore the T-shirt's bright fabric apart with ease and Jack quickly wrapped the fragment around the rung of the ladder.

It was not much but the small marker could help him find the way out if required.

No-one would want to get lost down here – even with lights running along the walls at random places.

Jack began a slow jog in his chosen direction. He counted slowly to try to give him an idea of how far he'd gone.

The ladder was soon lost behind him as Jack increased the pace.

At roughly 1,000 steps, he knew he'd chosen the right way.

The dull grinding sound was much louder now – like something being pulled along the floor – and was clearly ahead of him.

Jack could not see them yet but they were definitely there, somewhere in front, and he was closing the gap all the time.

When he reached 1,500 paces, Jack found a small cubbyhole built into the left wall of the tunnel.

It also had a ladder attached to the wall although it appeared to be far older than the one that he had used to climb down. Also, there was no light at the top that Jack could see.

The cubbyhole had a set of rough shelves carved into the side of the wall, which held a horde of treasures.

There was an antique lantern with a small candle inside, a half-empty box of matches and several jars of tinned food that were covered in cobwebs.

"Artie would still happily eat them," Jack snorted to himself.

Using the matches, he lit the lantern. The small flame was barely visible and added nothing to the light provided by the electric bulbs.

But, for some reason, the small flicker gave him strength.

Using the hatchet again, he cut off a longer strip from his T-shirt.

He tied the material to the wire holding the makeshift lights so it would act as another marker on the return journey.

Jack stepped back out of the cubbyhole, leaving the candle alight.

The sound ahead had become distant again. His brief distraction had cost valuable time.

He broke into a swift jog, watching the floor carefully to avoid slipping on the trickling water beneath his feet.

Jack could run. He was tall and wiry – his legs covered the ground in huge strides.

The brickwork and electric light bulbs flew past in a blur.

He lost count of the paces when he had passed the 2,000 figure.

It was a long way back to the first ladder, regardless of the actual number.

Jack paused for a second. Up ahead, the grinding had stopped. The tunnel curved ahead, which blocked his vision.

A distant knocking sound echoed around him.

Jack listened intently to try to identify the new sound, but it stopped immediately.

He began to run again but took care to make as little noise as possible.

Banging again. This time it was louder.

And it was followed by a deep creaking sound like something being wrenched open.

A door. Someone was opening a door.

They were leaving the tunnel, Jack realised with horror.

Moments later, the tunnel began to straighten out.

In the far distance, he could see shadows moving.

He had found them.

31. OPENING

Fitch stopped moving as the trailer came to an abrupt halt.

The binds around her ankles were nearly worn through, thanks to the constant rubbing against the sharp edge of the trailer.

Her legs ached with the effort but it would give her a fighting chance against these … monsters.

Yet the tunnel was now far quieter, apart from the faint buzz of the electric lights and the constant trickle of water.

But the lack of noise was a problem. If Fitch continued to grind through the restraints, then that Gillian woman might hear and all her work would have been for nothing.

She was unsure if she could kick her feet free from the frayed material – but she was definitely going to try.

"Fitch? What's happening?"

Stanley whispered the question even though he was facing the other direction.

Fitch wanted to hug the boy and tell him that everything was going to be OK.

With her wrists tied together, she could not even do that.

Instead she tried to soothe Stanley's nerves with a handful of carefully chosen words: "It is going to be fine, Stan the Man. Trust me…."

She did not get to finish the sentence.

Something hard whipped across Stanley's shoulder and Fitch's stomach with a loud crack, making both of them yelp in shock.

"Silence! No-one said you could talk."

Gillian.

Fitch's instincts had been correct: the old witch had been listening.

She muttered a quick prayer, grateful that she'd stopped attempting to break her bonds in the nick of time.

Gillian towered above them but had turned to face the other way, towards the tunnel wall.

Fitch shuffled to her left a tad to see what held the woman's interest – a dark iron door.

Knock.

Knock.

Knock.

The banging rang around the tunnel. The echo was louder here than earlier in the journey although it was impossible to know why.

"Come on. Come on.

"Where the hell are you, Ridgeon?"

Gillian was muttering to herself but she was close enough for Fitch to overhear every word.

Bang.

Bang.

Bang.

The woman's fist pounded on the door, which betrayed how angry she was.

Or was it nerves?

Fitch did not know but the more time she spent with this Gillian character, the more her intense dislike grew.

She had been clever, Fitch knew.

She had purposefully lured her into that house, using Stanley as bait, and Fitch had fallen for it – hook, line and sinker.

Fitch had never even seen the blow coming.

Heck, she hadn't even realised that evil woman was in the room until it was too late.

She only remembered turning at the very last moment as she became aware of the woman's presence, moments after she had crashed into Stanley and the bag with the strange light coming from it.

By then, it was too late.

Now they were at her mercy.

Gillian grabbed the walkie-talkie.

"Ridgeon. We are here, ready!"

The walkie-talkie crackled into life.

"Birch will be with you any second. Be ready."

Gillian screeched a response back.

"Birch!? Is he well enough? I need proper help here. My own strength will not be enough."

To Fitch, Gillian sounded like a woman on the edge.

And she was dangerously close to falling off completely.

The voice on the other end of the walkie-talkie, on the other hand, sounded completely relaxed and in control of the situation.

"Do not fret, he is fine. A little weak with only one working eye but Birch will be there any second.

"Trust me. Now get them inside and get this door sealed for good."

Right on cue, the iron door began to move.

With a groan, the rusty hinges began to turn as the door opened from the inside.

A huge man emerged into the tunnel, showing no sign of effort from having opened the hefty door.

A makeshift bandage – covered in a revolting green colour – had been wrapped over part of his head, leaving him with only one eye to see.

Fitch shivered as his eye ran over her and Stanley. This man was not friendly in the slightest.

Yet his appearance seemed to have a calming effect on Gillian.

She tapped the radio's button again.

"He is here. We will be with you in a few moments."

Fitch watched as Gillian dumped the radio in the trailer and moved towards the man with the bandaged head.

She spoke in a deathly whisper: "One of the rats has followed us down here.

"I heard him shouting a couple of minutes ago. Help me unload these two brats and then take care of him.

"It is time to drain the park of its floodwaters."

32. ESCAPE PLAN

The mud was thick and slimy.

It had been a fairly dry autumn but rain over the past few days had made the dirt soft enough to scrape up.

Artie worked furiously to coat the car in muck.

He was unsure if plastering a vehicle with mud counted as vandalism.

But he guessed it easily could.

"If this car doesn't belong to Ridgeon and his gang," the voice in his mind said, "then I am going to be in serious trouble."

But, deep down, he knew. It had to.

Why would anyone park a car in the middle of the woods? And bother to cover it up too?

Only those with something to hide, he reasoned with himself.

It was too much of a coincidence.

Artie wiped his dirty hands on to his jeans, which remained damp from the pond.

That seemed a very long time ago now. His mum would be beside herself by now. He pushed thoughts about his worrying mum firmly out of his mind. He had to focus.

Artie looked up the slope towards the spot where Berry had taken his last breath.

Ridgeon and the others would be coming through here to slip away before anyone knew what they'd done.

But Berry had unintentionally led him to the place where they would be at their weakest.

It was the perfect trap.

Artie could position himself carefully on the ridge, which overlooked the car – and wait for the goblin gang to arrive.

And then he would....

That was where his plan fell down.

He did not have a clue what to do next. For starters, he did not even know what direction they would be coming from.

Artie patted his back pocket to reassure himself that his phone was still there. It was there, much to his relief.

He gritted his teeth against the biting cold.

The temperature did not matter.

There would only be one chance at this.

He could not waste it.

Yet they outnumbered him three to one – at least – and he guessed they would be better prepared to deal with him this time.

Either way, he knew these evil creatures could not handle having bright lights shone in their eyes.

And this knowledge gave him the smallest chance to beat them.

He stood still, caught in two minds.

Where would they come from?

Should he stay nearer to the car?

There was no real path anywhere around here so how would they find their way?

Was there anything else he could do to stop their

escape?

The questions whirled around his mind.

And then he saw the answer. It was right in front of him yet somehow he had missed it the first time around.

The random planks of wood he had noted earlier had not been carelessly discarded as first thought.

Beside the thorny bushes and the timber stood a dark narrow entranceway, running deep into the mud.

The planks provided the frame for the doorway. Inside it was too dark to see far but there could be no doubt what it was.

A tunnel.

Artie's mind whirred relentlessly as he peered into the entrance.

It was more than a tunnel.

This was the escape route – and the car was the final step in the plan.

Artie made up his mind.

He pulled out his phone and switched the flashlight on.

The bright beam lit up his surroundings in a ghostly white colour.

There was only one thing to do.

He gulped down several lungfuls of fresh night air and took a final look at the car.

Satisfied the vehicle would not be going anywhere quickly, Artie turned and plunged into the darkness.

Whoever was planning to escape this way would have to get past him first.

Martin Smith

33. FLOOD

There was movement ahead.

Jack stuck solely to the shadows and slowed his approach. He had found them.

He began darting in and out of the darker patches between the electric lights in a zig-zag pattern.

This took more time but gave him the chance to get closer without giving his position away.

He wished he had not shouted without thinking when he was looking for Fitch and Stanley earlier.

Still, it had happened.

There was no way to change it now.

He just had to hope the loud grinding sound had somehow covered up his calls.

Jack estimated he was the length of two swimming pools away from the trailer.

Bodies were moving around but there did not appear to be many of them.

He pressed himself against the slimy brickwork, trying his best to stay invisible.

Now he had found them, he was unsure what to do next.

Should he go and challenge them?

Or should he try to sneak closer and help his friends escape?

The problem was he could not see either Fitch or Stanley.

And there were at least two adults up there – and he guessed neither of them would be friendly.

Jack risked another look, stepping into the light for a second before darting back to the safety of the shadows.

The trailer appeared to be empty.

A creaking sound of the door filled the confined space.

The wrenching sound echoed down the tunnel and finished with a loud thud.

Seconds later, the unmissable sound of a lock being turned into place reached Jack's ears.

His heart began to thud.

He was too late. Again. This was becoming a bad habit.

Forgetting the danger of the kidnappers, he ran in a crouch towards the trailer in desperation.

He was halfway there – about 25 metres or so – when another sound filled his ears.

Thud.

Thud.

Thud.

Jack could not see anyone ahead of him but the tunnel curved beyond the trailer, which stopped him seeing the source of the noise.

But someone was definitely still down here with him.

Hands curled into fists, Jack reached the back of the trailer and kneeled alongside the rear end, trying to remain hidden.

He had been right: the large metal door was now closed in the left-hand side of the tunnel.

Thud.

Thud.

The dull banging continued.

Jack decided to try the door. He was running out of options. Fitch and Stanley were there – on the other side.

He slipped. The trickle of water was greater here – it was flowing quickly over the ancient floor.

Jack picked himself up, wiped down his wet clothes, and moved to the doorway.

He was not surprised when the heavy barrier would not budge. Deep down, he knew it had been locked.

Thud.

Thud.

Jack left the door behind and crept nearer to the bend in the tunnel.

It was the only thing left.

His eyes stayed firmly on the floor. The incoming water was creating large puddles on the floor, making it tricky to walk safely.

Thud.

Thud.

Cat-like, Jack leapt over one puddle and silently merged into the shadows on the right-hand side of the tunnel.

It gave him a clear view of what was causing the noise.

His heart began to pound.

A giant of a man stood with his back to Jack, facing the tunnel's end.

He was only 10 metres away and worked with a giant sledgehammer, smashing into the bricks that blocked the tunnel.

Every time he landed a blow, a new spring of water erupted from the weakened wall.

Jack looked down. Water was now covering most of the floor.

Thud.

The man smashed the wall again and part of the barrier crumbled. Water began gushing in.

The man turned briefly and wickedly smiled in Jack's direction. Jack froze. How could he possibly know that he was there?

The giant had a bandaged head that looked a funny colour of green in the dim light.

He had a rope tied around his waist, which was attached to the wall.

He turned away and raised the mallet again.

Thud.

The next blow landed and the leaks of water burst out from numerous points.

Jack did not need to see any more.

This crazy guy was going to flood the tunnel.

And there was no way out.

Martin Smith

34. LAIR

The room looked like a standard living room.

There was a lamp in the corner and a flat-screen TV in another.

A couple of sofas and a sideboard made up the rest of the furniture.

It was completely normal – except there were no personal touches, Fitch realised.

No photos of family.

Not one picture hanging on the walls.

There were no ornaments on the windowsills or keepsakes of cherished memories on shelves.

It was supposed to look like a family home – except it wasn't.

This was a lair.

Fitch shuddered at the thought.

The big man with the bandaged head had easily lifted her and Stanley out of the trailer and through the wide door in the tunnel.

Several flights of stairs later, they had emerged inside this house, where they had been dumped on the living room floor

The man disappeared immediately, leaving her and Stanley alone.

"Don't worry, buddy. We're going to get out of this mess, I promise you. I won't let anything happen to you."

To her surprise, Stanley smiled: "I know, Finny. I am always safe when I'm with you.

"I am sorry. This is all my fault. She … tricked me. I know I should not have gone into that house but she said.…"

Stanley's voice tailed off as his smile disappeared.

"It's OK, Stanley. It's not your fault," she said kindly.

The younger boy shook his head. "Yes, it is. You said to me not to leave your sight and I forgot. That woman told me her name was Gillian.

"She said she thought my costume was the best she had seen all night and she had a really special prize for me."

Fitch began to interrupt but realised Stan needed to talk about what had happened. She stayed quiet instead.

He continued: "She said I would need to go inside because if any other children saw the prize, they would come rushing over too and she only had enough for very special kids.

"I asked if there was enough for you too and she said there would be.

"I stepped inside and she pulled the pumpkin in after me. She said she would be out of sweets once we had ours so there could be no more trick or treating.

"She asked how old I was. I told her and then she disappeared up the stairs, leaving me waiting in the hall.

"I could hear her talking to someone up there – talking about me and my age. I was beginning to get nervous and decided to come back to you but she returned and locked the door so I couldn't leave."

Stanley's words began to come out quicker as he remembered what had happened. Fitch's hands were still tied in front of her but she placed them on his arm.

She spoke gently: "Go on. What happened then."

Stanley took a breath: "She carried this box down the stairs – the one that you knocked over. The one that was glowing.

"Gillian said the magic bars of chocolate were inside it but I needed to go into the lounge to open it.

"She had this box with an odd … shine, I guess … coming from it and put it on the floor.

"I was just getting the bars out of the box when you came in … and everything went crazy."

A tear rolled down his nose and fell on the carpet.

"I am so sorry, Fitch.

"I know you should never trust a stranger. It is just it is Halloween and …"

Fitch gripped his arm.

"You're right to never trust strangers. I hope you've learned your lesson! But don't.…"

Fitch stopped talking. There were voices nearby.

One was Gillian's.

The other was male but it was not the same voice as the big guy who had carried them in. It was someone else – probably the man on the radio.

Stanley whispered.

"Who are these people, Fitch?

"And what do they want with us?"

Fitch shrugged.

"I don't know. Let's listen and try to…."

Gillian and the other male walked in.

The man's deep voice boomed out. He sounded like a dog. With a big smile, he clapped his hands together with excitement.

"Well done Gillian. This is excellent work. I can't believe that you have managed to pull it off. We can live off this for another year or two at least!

"How old is the boy? Nine?"

Fitch watched Gillian shake her head.

"He is seven, Ridgeon."

The man gasped.

"Wonderful. How you did it, I don't know.

"I take my hat off to you. The other one looks a little old but she will be a tasty starter."

Fitch thought she might be sick. Either she had misread their intentions … or they actually wanted to eat them.

Something was very wrong here.

The man's eyes were dancing with glee. He rubbed his hands together. He looked like he might break into a dance of celebration at any moment.

In his hand was a large kitchen knife, which glinted when the light caught the blade.

He stopped suddenly and spoke with a frown: "Where is Birch?"

Gillian tilted her head towards the direction of the stairs. "We had some … unexpected … company. Birch is currently taking care of that.

"He will meet us at the house on Flamingo Drive as we leave."

Fitch's heart jumped as she realised they were talking about Jack. She strained a little to test the ties around her ankles.

They were loose. She could break them – when the time was right.

Ridgeon scratched his crooked nose and ran a hand through his thin white hair.

"Very well. Let's get these moved to the car and take them to the safe house. Berry has missed the cut-off time."

Gillian grabbed the man's arm.

"Well then, we have to wait. We can't leave him out there. He won't make it alone."

Fitch could see the alarm on her face. It was the first time she had shown any sort of emotion apart from anger.

The older man patted her hand gently.

"No. Everyone knows the rules. The return time could not be missed.

"We have not seen him since … that shriek we heard as we helped Birch. I fear for him, but I will not put the rest of us in danger by waiting for Berry."

Gillian's eyes narrowed. "Was it … that boy?"

Fitch knew who they meant – only Artie Eason could drive people mad like that.

The older man continued unaware Fitch was listening to every word:

"Perhaps. Who knows? I suspect Berry was badly hurt during the chase – just like Birch had been.

"If only we had not rushed out without our glasses. I panicked and did not think it through. One mistake has cost us dearly."

The man stopped talking abruptly.

He paused for a moment and then sighed.

"Only your quick thinking saved Birch. But Berry was not close enough for us to help.

"I searched for him briefly but the trail was patchy and time has been against us.

"For a moment earlier in the night, I thought this was going to be a repeat of last year."

Licking his lips, he cast an eye over Fitch and Stanley.

He smiled wickedly: "Instead of last year's famine though, a feast awaits."

Gillian interrupted: "Where are your glasses, Ridgeon? We will need to have them to get through the tunnel."

Without looking, the man waved a hand randomly towards the other side of the house.

"Upstairs in the front bedroom. I removed them while I was keeping watch to ensure there has been no police activity outside. Thankfully, it appears we are in the clear."

Gillian walked to the door. "I'll get them. We cannot take any more risks – after what has happened tonight."

Ridgeon nodded. "Good idea. Thank you.

"Then we shall load the older one into the car first and then return for the boy afterwards.

"We cannot take risks with him. He is too precious."

Gillian disappeared without another word. Her footsteps quickly faded as she headed upstairs.

The man called Ridgeon stepped over Fitch and grabbed her roughly by the arm and leg to pick her up.

Without a word and using every bit of strength she had, Fitch's legs ripped out of the bonds and kicked the monster square in the chest.

35. SINKING

Water had reached Jack's knees.

He was frantically wading through the freezing swell, using every ounce of strength he had.

But it was a losing battle.

The water continued to swirl around him, rising higher up his body as every moment passed.

It was almost pitch black.

The handful of lights hung along the wall had disappeared moments after he had begun running.

A dim light flickered in the far distance, which Jack was aiming for.

Jack had no choice but to use his hands to guide him along the tunnel wall. It was slow going.

The teenager could not stop his teeth from chattering.

His hands began to shake with the cold. His heart was beating wildly.

A sound erupted behind him: the wall was collapsing.

The man had succeeded. Gallons of water poured immediately into the small space and echoed around the tunnel.

Jack felt panic rise inside him.

Such a fierce rush of water would fill the narrow tunnel in a matter of minutes.

And once it reached the curved ceiling, there would be nowhere left for him to breathe.

His only chance was to reach the ladder that he had used earlier to climb down here.

But that ray of hope was a long way off.

He had stopped counting the paces when he reached about 2,000 steps – and he had not even had a glimpse of the trailer at that point.

Jack guessed the iron door – the one Fitch and Stanley had vanished behind – had been perhaps more than 3,000 steps along the tunnel.

If only he had moved quicker, he could have saved them.

Now his friends were on their own in the clutches of these crazy people.

And he could not save them … because he was in grave danger too.

He estimated it would take 20 minutes or so to retrace his steps and reach the safety of the ladder.

It was time he did not have. Even with his running skills, he might make it halfway – perhaps.

The sound was becoming louder, closing in on him.

Jack risked a look over his shoulder as the deafening roar made it impossible to think about anything else.

He could not see anything but he could sense the huge wall of water crashing towards him.

Jack tried to increase his speed but it was too late.

The torrent was upon him.

It swept his legs out from under him, forcing his whole body underneath the freezing water.

Jack gasped in shock and swallowed in mouthfuls of dirty liquid.

He tumbled forwards – bowled over by the forceful momentum of the wave – and thrashed around to try to return to the surface.

His cheek scraped the side of the tunnel as the wave dragged him along without hesitation.

Desperately, Jack kicked his legs to escape the wave and smashed his head on the brick roof of the tunnel.

Choking for air and half stunned, he fell to the floor as the initial surge passed.

Jack found a footing and planted his feet.

He clung to the damp wall as he coughed and spluttered the water out of his aching lungs.

Cold and tired, Jack wanted to rest. Every breath hurt and the cold sent vicious chills through his body that he could not stop. His face stung and the palms of his hands were red raw.

Yet he could not stop. That would mean death.

The swirling torrents continued to rise. He would soon be out of time.

He would not last long in this tunnel. He had to get to the ladder.

The dim light that he spotted earlier was now much brighter. The powerful wave had dragged him a long way down the tunnel.

The lantern in the cubbyhole.

Jack felt hope soar within him.

It was much closer than the ladder – and he would be able to at least escape the rapids until the flood waters subsided.

Did it have a ladder there? Jack could not remember. Still, the small cupboard could prove to be his saviour.

He had no idea why he'd decided to light the lantern. Something inside his gut had told him to.

Now he was so grateful.

He waded towards the small beacon, which was burning brighter with every step he took.

By now, the water was lapping around his waist but Jack no longer felt cold. He was going to get out of this mess.

He found bouncing along – rather than simply running – helped his momentum, similar to the astronauts who walked on the moon.

The lantern beam glimmered off the gushing torrents.

Jack breathed a huge sigh of relief as he stepped into the small zone of light, projecting from the cubbyhole.

He turned his body sideways and shuffled across the tunnel towards the safety of the small nook.

It was harder moving across the water rather than travelling with the direction of the current.

But, with a final heave, his hands grasped the small rungs of the cubbyhole and he lugged himself partly out of the water.

He had never been more grateful to see a lit candle. Guided by its flickering glow, he could make out the outline of a ladder heading upwards.

He had done it.

Jack climbed on to the first rung of the ladder, hauling more of his body away from the cold current. The air felt tropical.

He felt exhausted as he looked at the small candle,

basking in the tiny amount of heat coming from its flickering flame. His head throbbed but he did not care: he had made it.

The rungs continued upwards but he could still not see if there was an exit at the top or not.

Jack had no choice. He had to try to climb up there and get help. His friends were still in danger, after all.

Taking a deep breath, his fingers stretched towards the next step of the ladder.

But he never reached it.

Out of nowhere, a huge hand grabbed his ankle and a firm tug sent Jack plunging back into the swirling depths below.

36. FIGHT

Fitch's foot hit Ridgeon square in the chest and sent him flying into the wall behind him.

Eyes open wide with surprise, the savage blow caught the man off balance.

He toppled over and could not stop falling backwards into the brickwork with a loud thud. The knife fell out of his hand, away from his clutches.

Ridgeon sank to his knees and tried to regain his senses, reeling from the unexpected attack.

Fitch knew this was her chance.

She had run the situation over and over in her mind but never dared to believe her kick would pack such power.

For a split second, she considered scooping up the boy in her arms and making a dash for it.

But her arms were still tied. Stanley still had both his arms and feet bound together.

She could not run far while carrying him.

They would be caught before they got out of the house.

"Gillian! Gillian!"

Wheezing deeply, Ridgeon did not have enough air in his lungs to shout loudly to his accomplice. It was not loud enough for her to hear – yet.

The first plea for help came out as a mere whisper but he would soon regain his breath.

This was it.

Fitch struggled to her feet, frustrated that her balance was affected by the binds around her wrists.

"You little...." Ridgeon snarled at her from across the room with spittle flying from his lips.

Two strides were enough to close the gap between them and leave her standing above the man who had tried to kidnap her.

A swift boot to the groin sent Ridgeon sprawling on to the floor. She followed the blow with another brutal kick to the stomach.

The man curled into a ball to limit the impact of the kicks.

Fitch heard a sound coming from upstairs.

Time was short. That awful woman would be back soon.

She had to get Stanley safe.

She stepped over Ridgeon's body on the floor and picked up the knife that he dropped. A flash of the blade saw her binds drop harmlessly to the floor.

She dashed to the window.

It was locked.

The handle would not budge an inch.

Her eyes flickered across the other window locks. It was a large window, looking out on to the front garden of the house.

There!

In the third and furthest lock sat a grimy silver key, no bigger than a long fingernail.

Fitch grabbed it and tried to thrust the key into the lock of the central window.

It wouldn't go in.

She realised it was her shaking hands that were stopping the key entering the lock.

"Calm down. Calm down. You can do this."

Fitch repeated the words over and over as she tried to bring her ragged breathing under control.

The strange smell in the house – similar to the awful pong that had plagued them in the tunnel – did not help.

She tried to block it out along with everything else.

And, when she tried again, the key slid in first time.

"Yes!"

Her heart leapt as the large window swung open and the fresh air of the October night flooded in.

She turned back to Stanley.

The banging was getting closer. She did not have time to cut his bonds too so she flung the kitchen knife on to the nearby couch.

Instead, with an almighty heave, she picked up the boy and placed him on the window sill.

"Stanley, listen to me. I'm going to lower you out of here. It is not far down.

"Once you get outside, hide.

"Find somewhere dark. Do not make a sound for anyone. Do you understand?"

Tears trickled down his face.

Fitch shook him.

"Don't cry, Stan the Man. Don't be upset. Be the brave champion that I know you are. It is going to be fine. I will follow you out of here straight away, I promise."

She wiped the fresh tears away falling freely from his young face.

"I promise you that I will follow. Now … move.

"Swing those legs out of here and I'll keep hold of you to make sure you don't fall."

Stanley did as he was told.

As soon as his legs dropped on to the ground, he twisted around and his small body slipped easily through the window.

Fitch kept hold of him until she was completely sure that he was steady on his feet.

"Gillian! Help!"

Ridgeon croaked the words again.

Surely Gillian would be coming back at any second?

Fitch knew time was short.

"Over there!" Fitch pointed towards a large clump of bushes to Stanley's right – and watched him begin to shuffle in the right direction.

Fitch felt a weight lift from her shoulders. Stanley was going to be safe. No-one would find him in the darkness.

Now she needed to raise the alarm and get the police to deal with these monsters.

A house with a long driveway across the road had lights on both upstairs and downstairs.

She would aim for there – and planned to knock on the door and plead with the people living there to help her.

Fitch took a giant stride and planted a foot on the window sill as she prepared to jump.

Two strong hands grabbed her neck and pulled her back into the house, which sent Fitch tumbling to the floor.

She squealed with pain as she collapsed awkwardly on one of her knees.

Ridgeon kneeled next to her and grunted with the

effort, his face a picture of rage. His carefully slicked back hair had become wild and ragged. His eyes were ablaze.

"No, you don't, Missy. You'll be staying here."

His hands went to her throat and began to squeeze.

Fitch kicked out and desperately tried to pry the fingers from her neck.

But the grip got even tighter.

Fitch scratched and kicked out but was not strong enough to stop him.

Black spots began to float in front of her eyes. Her lungs burned with the lack of air.

Fitch knew it was over. They had beaten her. At least Stanley was safe.

Out of nowhere, Ridgeon screamed loudly and let her go.

Fitch choked as oxygen flooded back into her body, unsure why the monster had released his grip.

And then another voice spoke loudly – one she knew only too well.

"Get off her."

37. DARKNESS

Ice-cold water filled his ears, nose and mouth.

Jack's head crashed into the far wall as he tried to rise to the surface to suck in some air.

Ignoring the pain, he used his feet to push himself upwards into the air above.

As the water level kept rising, that lifeline was getting smaller. He could not stay in the tunnel much longer.

He had no idea how the giant man had closed the gap between them so quickly – or was able to keep his footing in such slippery conditions.

Yet here he was.

He was super strong too. Jack was no wimp but he knew the man was far stronger than him.

If it came down to a straight fight, there would only be one winner.

The teenager had one option: escape the tunnel – and the man who the woman had called Birch earlier – before the filthy water filled it completely.

Jack could not see where the man was but he must be close.

Twisting and turning, Jack fought against the freezing water to stop himself plunging into the deeper depths of the tunnel.

He felt a sharp pain in his thigh.

The hatchet.

Its blade had cut part of his upper leg when he had been yanked out of the cubbyhole.

He pulled the axe out of his trouser waistband and clutched it in his right hand.

It was not much of a weapon but it was better than nothing. Teeth chattering, he risked a glimpse back up the tunnel.

The light of the lantern was now merely a distant flicker. It was long gone.

And somewhere between him and that escape route was the man.

A shadow moved followed by a splashing sound. The noise was getting louder – Birch was closing in again.

He had no choice: the cubbyhole was no longer an option. The flow of the current meant he could only go forwards, not back.

Jack took a final look at the flicker of light and took a deep breath.

Then he dived under the surface and began to swim as fast as he could – into the darkness.

Jack had always been a strong swimmer.

Many early mornings had been spent in the decaying Foston pool training for local swimming galas.

Never in his wildest dreams did he think that training would save his life under the ground.

But here he was.

He swam under the water, only surfacing now and again to take deep breaths.

Swimming with the flow of the water meant he shot along although several times he collided with the sides of the tunnel as it curved left and right.

He had not meant to zig-zag across the tunnel but, with no light to guide him, it was the best he could do.

When he could no longer see the flickering light from the lantern, he changed to breaststroke and swam with his head fully above the water with an arched back.

It was slower but he could not afford to swim past the second ladder.

If he missed that ladder then he really would be in trouble, mainly because he had absolutely no idea of what else lay down the other end of the tunnel.

A fresh light lit the tunnel walls ahead of him. The hefty beam was going straight over his head, coming from somewhere behind him.

Still swimming, Jack twisted his neck to what it was.

The man was carrying a powerful torch and was using it to scan side to side, searching for Jack.

For the moment, the teen was out of the spotlight but it would not take long for the man to find him.

Amazingly, he was only about ten metres behind him. Jack could not believe the speed the man was travelling.

How was he doing it?

The beam flashed above his head again and Jack spotted the tell-tale flash of red in the distance.

His ripped fragment of T-shirt still clung to the bottom rung of the ladder.

Jack's heart leapt.

He was going to make it.

The torch beam went out and the tunnel plunged back into darkness.

It did not matter.

Jack kicked out with fresh determination to reach the target that was now so tantalisingly close.

Ten metres.

Five.

Two.

One.

His hand reached out and his fingers grabbed the rung.

With a big heave, he lugged part of his aching body into the welcoming warm air.

The tunnel suddenly became bathed with light once more.

Jack slipped in panic.

Birch was now less than 20 metres away from him – and closing fast.

38. FREEDOM

Artie Eason stood in the doorway.

His eyes scanned the room, looking down at the evil goblin that had imprisoned his best friend and little brother.

"This ends tonight. You will pay for this."

Ridgeon snarled.

"You! The little sneaky rat!"

"No, you are mistaken. It is you who will pay this time!"

Before Artie could stop him, Ridgeon bellowed at the top of his voice: "GILLIAN! IT'S HIM.

"THE RAT IS HERE. HE'S BACK."

From his crouched position on the floor, the goblin suddenly threw himself at Artie in a wild rage.

Yet Artie was ready. He'd expected a sneaky attack and was waiting for it.

His knee connected sweetly with Ridgeon's chin and sent the monster back to the ground with a howl of pain.

Eyes blazing, Artie stepped fully into the lounge, calmly closed the door and ignored the crazed goblin's taunts.

He held his mobile in front of him as a warning to stop the goblin from trying to attack him again.

Fitch moaned from the floor but he could not understand the words.

He knelt beside his friend.

She seemed to not be hurt too badly, a little groggy. Artie did not want to even begin to think about what she had been through.

He spoke gently: "Ssshhh, Fitch. It is OK. You're safe now. I'm here."

He looked around the room again.

"Where is Stan?"

Fitch gestured towards the window.

"Safe. He is hiding – out there."

Artie followed her nod and saw a shadow fall across the glass.

Stanley must have heard his voice.

Artie gave a thumbs-up to show that he had understood before standing up and returning his attention to Ridgeon once more.

The goblin had crawled to the door and was trying to reach the door handle but seemed in too much pain to stand.

He was not a threat at the moment.

Gillian may still be a problem but Artie had his phone and, besides, he was finished running away from these monsters.

This goblin would pay for his crimes, and so would his friends.

Artie did not know how many children these creatures had attempted to steal over the years but it would not continue.

The police could question Ridgeon and find out exactly how far their wicked plans went.

But they would not be hurting anyone else.

Artie carried the wire that Birch dumped on the

dining room table several hours earlier.

Fitch got to her feet slowly. She rested against one of the chairs. Slowly the colour began to return to her cheeks.

Artie thrust his phone towards her.

"If this creep moves or Gillian comes in, smash the flashlight on and shine it directly in their faces.

"It burns them."

Fitch raised her eyebrows.

She whispered: "Why don't we just ring the police?"

Artie did not have time to explain further about the mobile jamming.

"I'll explain everything later."

His hands moved quickly to tie Ridgeon firmly in place. The wire was strong and would not break.

The goblin spat and snarled as he was trussed up securely but he could not stop them.

Soon it was done.

The leader of the goblin gang had been captured. Another one was already dead.

The others would be rounded up soon enough.

And Ridgeon would soon be in the hands of the police, who could dish out the suitable punishment.

Fitch frowned: "Where's the woman?"

Artie could tell Fitch was nervous about Gillian.

He shook his head: "No idea. She moved upstairs at the same time as I came in. I'm going to get Stanley – where is he again?"

Fitch replied but did not dare to take her eyes off Ridgeon.

"He's out there in one of the bushes. I was just following him out when this … man … stopped me."

Artie placed a hand on her shoulder.

"I know. You've been amazing. We are nearly there, I promise you. I'll get Stanley. We can't leave him out there alone.

"Everything is going to be all right."

Artie squeezed her shoulder and vaulted out of the open window with barely a second thought.

He turned and saw Fitch standing over the goblin, holding the phone out as a threat.

Happy that Fitch had the situation under control, he switched his attention back to finding his little brother.

He called out: "Stanley? Where are you, buddy?"

No response.

Artie crept closer to the nearby bushes that Fitch had indicated that Stanley was hiding in.

The street lights provided just enough light to tell Artie that there was no-one there.

"Stan? It's me, Artie. You can come out now," he spoke a little louder.

No response.

He stopped and looked around. Where had he gone?

"Stan!"

At last, the response came.

The sound was muffled and came from a distance away but it was definitely Stanley – and the words chilled Artie to the bone.

"Fitch! Artie! Anyone! Help! Help me … please."

39. LIGHTS OUT

"Fitch! Close this window behind me and let's go.

"She's got Stanley and making a run for it – we have got to move, right now!"

Artie scrambled back through the window and grabbed his phone from a startled-looking Fitch.

The phone only had seven per cent of its battery remaining. He hoped it would be enough.

Fitch looked stunned: "Artie, what? How…."

Ridgeon began to laugh.

It was a cruel, horrible sound.

"You fools! She is far too clever for the likes of you.

"Your brother will be the child that saves the goblin race.

"Do you have any idea how much imagination a seven-year-old boy has? We can feast for weeks on his mind!

"We can survive on your imaginations, of course, but the magic has gone by the teenage years.

"Any imagination is replaced with a need for sleep and a craving for drama during those horrible years!

"We got lucky tonight and we would never give up on a prize like Stanley so easily. And this is your fault, my dear."

The goblin grinned with spite as Fitch slammed the window shut, trying to ignore him.

He gloated: "Sending him outside alone, thinking it was safer.

"Oh, my dear, that was extremely stupid – a little bit like sending a poor lamb into the lion's den."

Fitch looked as if she was about to cry.

"What's he talking about, Artie? Why do they want our imaginations? How is that even possible?"

Ridgeon cackled again.

"Oh, this is so wonderful. You haven't told her, have you Art?

"You were so busy trying to save everyone that you forgot to tell your very best friends about our wonderful plans!"

Artie pulled the phone of his pocket and held it close to Ridgeon's eyeball.

"No-one calls me 'Art'.

"One more word from you and I'll light you up. Understand, slime ball?"

The smile had slipped from Ridgeon's face.

Artie's face was like thunder.

"Do you understand?"

Ridgeon gave the smallest of nods and turned his head away from the menace of the phone.

Fitch began to speak but Artie stopped her.

They did not have the time. He would explain everything when they were moving.

Artie double-checked the wire bonds that held Ridgeon.

They were secure.

There would be no escape for him.

He then attached the wire to the door handle to make certain that Ridgeon was going nowhere.

"Come on, Fitch, this way.

"The good news is that they're heading through the woods – but, luckily for us, I know a quicker route."

Taking Fitch's hand, they darted through the house, grabbing the walkie-talkie from the dining room table as they went.

But, instead of leaving via the back door as Fitch expected, they stopped in front of the small hallway cupboard.

Artie yanked the flimsy door open.

Fitch gasped with shock as a series of wooden steps leading down into darkness were revealed.

"Another tunnel?"

Artie nodded.

"Yes, they were planning to move everyone across town using the old underground tunnel system. This is their own extension to it.

"I know exactly where Gillian is going.

"She is heading for the far end of this tunnel but it is dark and she won't know the way through the woods.

"We can still catch them – if we're really quick."

Fitch put a hand on her head. "Artie. I need some answers before we go anywhere. I'm … scared."

Artie hesitated.

Every second counted but he knew that his friend had been through hell and back during the past couple of hours.

She had been incredibly brave – showing more strength than he thought possible from anyone – but he needed just a little bit more from her.

He spoke softly: "I know. I am too. Let's catch them up and rescue Stanley.

"Then I'll explain everything. The goblins, the nosebleeds, the imagination grabbing."

Fitch's eyes widened a touch.

"Goblins?" she whispered. "You're telling me…."

Artie nodded.

"The tale is long and quite incredible.

"Yes, these … people … creatures … they are actual goblins. Not how we have ever imagined them or like we've seen in the movies.

"And, although I'm not quite sure exactly why, they need to eat our imaginations if they want to survive."

Fitch clutched his arm.

"What are you talking about? That sounds … sick."

Artie gently peeled her hand off his forearm.

"I know. It is completely crazy but we don't have the time to talk about it all now. Trust me – I will tell you all I know.

"Everything we have gone through will have been a waste if we don't get my little brother back right now.

"He needs us … and I need you. Let's do this."

He did not wait for a response.

Artie opened the precious flashlight on his phone and strode into the tunnel.

He was soon swallowed by the darkness.

Fitch followed moments later.

There was no time to waste. Stanley needed them.

40. GETAWAY

It was like a nightmare that Stanley couldn't wake up from.

A rag had been tied around his mouth as soon as he had cried out to his brother.

The boy could not shout for help again.

Dark shapes flashed by as the woman lugged him through the woods at speed.

He wanted to cry.

He had done exactly as Fitch had told him and hid in the big bush next to the house, as quiet as a mouse.

But Fitch had not followed him outside like she had promised.

And that devil woman had found him instead.

He had not even seen her coming.

Her long fingers – that reminded Stanley of a spider – had slipped around his neck before he could shout a warning.

Then with surprising strength, she picked him up and flung him over her shoulder. For some strange reason, she was wearing sunglasses.

His hands and feet were still tied up from earlier. They felt numb.

In her other hand, Gillian carried a small brown

leather bag that she always kept close to her. He had seen it earlier too.

Stanley groaned with every step they took. He bounced up and down on the woman's bony shoulder, which hurt his stomach.

She ignored the moans and concentrated fully on finding the correct path through the dark woodland.

Stanley had no idea where they were going but the houses were soon left behind – and, with them, the lights.

Deeper and deeper, they careered into the dark night.

His tummy was becoming more painful with every step.

Without warning, she stopped and let him slip off her shoulder without a second glance.

Stanley landed on the floor with a thud.

Then the smell hit him.

The ground was wet but it was the stink that upset him.

It was disgusting. Stanley had never smelt anything like it before.

He tried not to breathe – to stop the horrible odour wafting into his nostrils.

But he could not last long.

Lungs bursting, he finally took a breath in.

The air reeked.

It was a stink that he could not describe. It made him feel ill.

Stanley turned his head to the side but the stink remained.

He wriggled on to his back and the air here – away from the ground – was a little fresher.

As he lay on the floor, he could hear Gillian

mutter: "Oh Berry, you silly idiot. Why did you have to be so brave?

"We would have all survived handsomely.

"If only you could see the prize that I have picked up."

Stanley shivered. Prize?

What prize?

Trying to ignore the smell, Stanley kept a close eye on the woman.

Keeping her brown bag close to her side, she was kneeling over a pile of old clothes … and nothing else.

"She's lost her mind. There's no-one here called Berry – that's just some old clothes. Was she going crazy?" thought Stanley as he shivered at the biting cold.

Moments later, Gillian picked herself up, grabbed Stanley around the scruff of the neck and dragged him to his feet.

With a flash of a hidden blade, she cut the bonds that tied his legs.

She snapped: "You can walk the rest of the way, boy. I am not carrying you another step.

"No funny business. I mean it. You can go first. Follow the light."

She pulled out a torch and clicked the button.

Nothing happened.

"Stupid thing!" Gillian thumped the torch hard against her leg and a weak beam leaked out.

Stanley did not argue.

He was glad to be away from the ghastly smell, even if it did seem to linger on his skin.

The small pile of discarded, muddy clothes soon disappeared from view as they moved down a long slope.

Gillian walked closely behind him: the torch in one hand and the bag in the other.

They moved slowly as the torch struggled to produce enough light to see more than three metres ahead of them.

Stanley could hear the occasional rumble of a car – so he knew they must be near a main road.

Yet the darkness seemed to be so thick you could almost touch it.

"You … useless.…"

The torch had died and Gillian exploded in rage.

He stood still, now unable to see his hand in front of his face.

"Absolute amateurs. I told them.…"

Stanley kept looking ahead as he heard the torch being flung with anger back into the woods.

Gillian removed her glasses and stuffed them deep into her jacket pocket: "I hardly need these at the moment, do I?

"Keep moving forwards. I know exactly where we are going."

This time she moved with her spare hand on Stanley's shoulder, guiding him through the woods.

Stanley felt exhausted.

He was unsure what time it was but, from the darkness, he guessed it was late – way past his bedtime. He was cold and hungry.

He just wanted to go home.

Onwards they moved but now at an even slower pace.

They edged down the muddy slope and skirted past a huge black bush, full of spiky thorns and brambles.

Stanley realised Gillian was looking for something.

Abruptly she yanked him to a halt. Stanley obeyed. He was too tired to do anything else.

"We're here."

It did not look any different from the other bushes, Stanley thought to himself, as they approached it.

And then he saw the glint of metal.

This was no bush. It was a car.

She was taking him away.

41. GONE

The phone's battery was down to four per cent. It would automatically close itself down when the two per cent marker was reached.

It would not last much longer.

"Hurry Fitch! We're nearly there!"

The pair of them had raced down the tunnel as quickly as they could.

It was tight and cramped but it was big enough for the friends to be able to jog without banging their heads.

"They made this place?"

Fitch was a few paces behind.

She had been anxious over whether the handmade tunnel would be safe – but had been impressed by how solid it was.

Artie answered without looking back.

"Yeah, a guy called Birch made it. He was an evil man – he was like their henchman. I took care of him though."

Fitch did not respond for a moment.

"Wait … this Birch fella. Was he huge? I mean … bigger than almost anyone you've ever seen before?"

Artie replied: "Yep – that's the one. How do you know that?"

Fitch came to a dead halt: "Oh no. No! No! No! He has gone after Jack. Artie, we have to do something."

Artie kept running for a couple of seconds before realising Fitch was no longer following.

"Jack? What? How could he? I hurt him, really badly. I did the same thing to him as I did to Berry and he...."

Artie tailed off, unable to finish the sentence.

Fitch approached him slowly.

"He had been hurt. He was wearing a thick bandage around his head, but he was alive.

"He carried Stanley and me into the house. And then that awful witch sent him to hunt down Jack."

Fitch's hands curled into fists.

"Jack had been trying to save us. He had followed us all the way from the pumpkin house.

"And now it's just the two of them down there. Oh god, Artie, we need to help him!"

Artie gripped both her hands.

"No, Fitch. We need to get Stanley first. Jack is big and bad enough to look after himself.

"Come on. We're nearly there. The end of the tunnel is just up ahead. It's where they are heading.

"They have a car there. It's all part of their getaway plan.

"They wanted to smuggle you and Stan along here, away from prying eyes, except we managed to mess the whole thing up!

"Now let's go and get Stan and make sure these creatures can never do this kind of thing again!"

The phone beeped. Suddenly they were pitched into darkness.

"Artie?"

"Yes. My phone has just died. Our only weapon is useless. We can still save Stanley though. Follow me!"

They travelled slower without any light but Artie had been right: the tunnel's entrance was only a stone's throw away.

The pair emerged from the narrow space and gulped down the fresh air in the woodland.

Neither said it but both of them were glad to be free of the narrow tunnel walls and low ceiling.

Fitch whispered: "Where are we?"

Artie did not answer.

His eyes were fixed on the dull light ahead of them.

"Let's go. If we keep quiet, then we can sneak up on them without her even knowing."

They ran in a half-crouch towards the light, which came from lamp posts in the distance.

The car quickly came into view. The engine was running but it was not moving.

The driver's door was open.

Artie allowed himself a small smile.

His earlier meddling had paid off – they had not been able to get away.

Gillian was trying to clear the mass tangle of branches and mud off the windscreen that he had plastered there earlier.

They could hear her chuntering away about the unexpectedly terrible state of the car.

There was no sign of Stanley. He was either tied up on the back seat or in the boot.

Fitch crouched beside him.

"What shall we do?"

Artie rubbed his chin. He wanted to tackle the old witch head on but, without the phone, he wasn't sure how to do it.

"We need to create a distraction so I can rush her."

Fitch puffed out her cheeks.

"This woman is evil. I mean it, Artie. She is the worst of the lot.

"She'll do anything to steal Stanley. Absolutely anything. We can't mess around with her.

"We've only got this one chance."

Artie listened carefully.

Fitch always seemed to understand people, far better than he ever did.

She was right – as usual. They needed to be clever. They still had the element of surprise and they could not waste it.

"That's a good point, Fitch. OK, I've got a plan."

42. CHANCE

Jack tried to block out the blinding light that was bearing down upon him.

His hands scrambled to grab the rungs of the ladder again as the water reached up to his neck.

One.

Two.

With a grunt, he climbed another step and began to pull himself out of the water once more.

He risked a quick look back along the tunnel and regretted it immediately.

Birch was now only ten metres away.

A rope was wrapped around his monstrous body, which was attached to the guiding line running along the wall.

This allowed Birch to travel quickly without ever crashing into either side of the tunnel.

It had kept him afloat too – meaning there was no danger that he would swept away with the strong current.

It had been no wonder that the man had closed the gap so quickly, particularly with his long legs.

Jack pulled himself up another step.

If he could get far enough up the ladder, he was sure he could win a climbing race against the giant man.

But he would need to have a decent head start because Birch had a long reach, as he had proved already.

He would simply drag the boy back into the dark water if he could grab him – and then Jack would be at his mercy.

With sudden burst of effort, he climbed another couple of steps. Only his knees and feet were still in the cold water.

He stole another look at Birch.

To his amazement, the man was smiling.

It was a wicked grin that stretched across his whole face.

The bandage across his head was soaked and looked bright green in the flashlight's glare.

His one eye seemed to dance around with delight as he got closer.

"Gotcha."

The word was spoken loudly.

And the meaning was clear.

Jack scrambled with a new urgency.

His feet stepped out of the water and on to the bottom rung, relieving the pressure on his exhausted arms.

His hopes soared.

But, just like earlier, an iron-like grip attached to his ankle.

In desperation, Jack wedged his arms between the rungs and wall.

He knew what was coming and was determined to hold on with all his might before the inevitable yank came.

It worked.

Birch may have been stronger but this time Jack did not tumble straight into the water like earlier.

Somehow, he managed to still hold on to the ladder although the man had not let go of his leg.

But it came at a price with his arm becoming awkwardly stuck.

"Arrrgghhh!"

Jack cried out in pain as Birch pulled again – with greater force this time.

"Come on, sunshine. Let's go for a nice swim."

It sounded like Birch was playing games.

Jack kicked out in panic but only swiped at thin air.

Both of the man's hands quickly snared around his right leg.

And this time Jack could not hold on completely.

He cried out in agony as the man's full weight yanked his body down and his left arm remained caught underneath the rung.

Jack screamed and wrestled to set his trapped arm free, partially falling into the water but still clinging to the ladder with his legs.

But the decision to let go had caught Birch off balance.

The giant tripped backwards and fell under the water, taking one of Jack's shoes with him.

For a moment, Jack thought the man had been swept away but then remembered he was attached to the wall with the rope.

Then he bobbed up for air, immediately beneath Jack.

The bandage had completely gone, revealing an ugly dark green-smear where his eye used to be.

Birch, it appeared, had been in the wars too.

He looked crazed, like a mad man.

Jack did not care. His left arm had been badly hurt. He could still move it but it would be little help if he had to climb quickly.

Options were becoming limited.

He could not outrun the man and there was no chance that he could win a fight between them.

"You can still out-think him," he told himself.

Out of nowhere, a plan sprang into his mind.

He did not have time to consider if it would work or not.

He was out of choices.

Using his injured arm to keep his balance on the ladder, Jack fished the hatchet out of his waistband and swung with all his might.

Birch saw the blow coming and ducked easily out of the way.

He smiled.

"Is that really the best you can do?" He spoke with a sneer.

The second blow was avoided with even more ease.

"You are a pathetic little wimp."

The third attempt was not even close.

Birch's strong hands reached out to drag the boy under the water for a final time.

Yet the goblin had misread Jack's intentions.

Jack had not been aiming at him at all.

His focus had been fully on the wall behind him.

Each blow had landed on the rope that kept Birch securely attached to the wall.

A look of confusion fell over the giant's face.

He felt the rope go slack as his safety net was

removed, the forceful current suddenly making him unbalanced.

Jack hissed: "Enjoy your swim, big guy."

He swung the hatchet a final time, close enough to force Birch to swerve out of the way.

And that was enough.

With a roar of surprise, Birch dived backwards to escape the sharp silver blade that flashed towards him.

But without being harnessed safely to the wall, he fell straight underneath the raging waters and was swept away.

Jack watched as the torch's beam quickly flickered out and Birch's cries of anger rapidly faded away.

The mad man was gone.

Jack was finally safe.

Martin Smith

43. LIGHT

Soapy water sprayed on to the windscreen and bounced away uselessly, leaving a fine mist hanging in the damp air.

Gillian let out another shriek of rage and thumped the steering wheel. Her neatly planned escape was taking too long.

Stanley could hear her cursing and yelling but did not understand half of the words.

She was mad though, angrier than he'd seen her all night.

He was scared. She had thrown him in the back seat along with the brown handbag and her sunglasses. He could not see out of either of the car's rear windows.

The boy's view was limited to the gap between the front two seats. Beyond that, the windscreen was a mess of mud and dirt.

The car was undriveable. Gillian kept jumping out to clear more of the muck off the glass.

Minutes passed and, inch by inch, the windscreen was beginning to clear.

Slowly at first and then with gathering speed, the layer of mud began to peel away as the screen-wash began to penetrate deeper.

Finally, Stanley could see a black hole out of the glass. Gillian continued to chunter in the driver's seat, although the clearing windscreen seemed to be calming her nerves.

She revved the engine. The motor purred like a cat that had been given a saucer of warm milk.

Stanley panicked. She was kidnapping him – and there was no-one coming to save him. Where was Fitch?

He kicked the door with both legs. Nothing happened.

He repeated the trick but got the same result.

Gillian twirled round in her seat. He felt as if her stare was going to burn on a hole right through his skull.

"Stop it, little rat. Or I'll chop off your feet and throw them out of the window."

Stanley stopped, not sure if she meant the threat or not. Either way, he did not want to risk it.

She cackled as the mud cleared even further.

"Right, off we go then. Nice and gently – and no-one will notice us disappearing."

The engine revved but they did not move.

"What now?"

She accelerated a little harder this time and the engine growled in response. The wheels spun underneath them but they remained rooted in the same spot.

"What the ..."

Gillian leapt out of the car again and disappeared from Stanley's view. He waited as he heard scuffling under the car.

He did not have to wait long. She leapt back in the driver's seat and bashed the steering wheel with both hands.

"We're stuck! We've sunk into this dratted mud. Blast it."

Gillian stopped talking as a shadow fell across the car. It was dark outside with barely any light but they both saw it.

As quick as a flash, the shadow was gone again. She flicked the windscreen wipers off.

The gentle hum of the engine was the only sound that could be heard.

Everything else was still.

"We need to get out of...."

Gillian never finished the sentence.

A rock – about the size of a cricket ball – crashed through the front passenger window.

Stanley closed his eyes as tiny shards of shattered glass covered him.

Moments later, a larger stone smashed into the rear windscreen with a loud thud.

This time, the glass did not shatter but it was now impossible to see out of the damaged back window.

"The little...."

She put her foot to the floor and the engine roared into life. Stanley felt the car move a fraction.

It happened again as the tyres found a smidgeon of grip.

Thud.

Another rock hit the car but it hit one of the door panels and fell away, harmlessly to the side.

"It looks like your pathetic friends are trying to save you!"

Gillian sounded like she had lost her mind. Stanley kept his eyes closed, trying to ignore her, although hope soared inside his mind at the thought of a rescue.

She shrieked: "Well, it is too late! I will not be denied. If they get in my way again, I will make sure they are sorry!"

The engine revved again and this time the car moved forward several steps.

He heard a click as Gillian strapped her seatbelt across her chest: "Ha! Yes, we are free! We are leaving, my little Stanley!"

With the car finally ready to move, she flicked on the car's powerful full beam lights to guide her through the rest of the woods and to the safety of the road below.

Stanley opened his eyes as the inside of the car unexpectedly became bathed in bright light.

To his surprise, Gillian screamed in agony.

He looked at the mud-splattered woman in the front of the car.

She was desperately trying to cover her eyes as the blinding light poured into the vehicle.

"My glasses! Where are my glasses? Pass them to me now!"

Stanley saw them. They were inches from his head on the back seat where she'd dumped them earlier.

Gillian hissed: "Where are they, little rat?"

Stan didn't answer. A swift flick of his cheek sent the pair of designer shades tumbling into the foot well, out of sight.

"Arrrggghhh!"

Gillian could no longer talk. Both of her hands clutched her face to shield it from the bright glare.

Stanley saw one of the doors open and gasped but it did not matter.

Gillian could not respond any more. She groaned and writhed in the driver's seat, trapped by the dazzling illumination.

Artie placed his grubby hands on Stanley's shoulders.

"Stanley. I've got you. You're safe, buddy. They can't hurt us anymore."

With a huge grunt, Stanley was pulled out of the car and on to the damp earth below.

Fitch was there too. They quickly cut the binds and gag that had left the small boy helpless.

"What are we going to do about her?"

The goblin continued to thrash inside the vehicle. Her screams were getting more desperate and a foul smell began to fill the air.

Artie shrugged: "She can't get out. We waited on purpose until she was strapped in until we made our move. It took ages too.

"If she tries to undo the seatbelt and get out, then the light will eat her up.

"She'll still be sitting there when the police arrive. It's finally all over, Stanley, I can promise you that."

44. MISSING

Artie was bored of being stuck in bed.

Every time he tried to leave his bedroom though, his mum had sent him back to bed.

Doctors at the hospital had been quite clear: he had been very lucky to escape the adventure with only a chesty cough

Complete rest and plenty of hot drinks had been recommended to his mum – and she was making sure they stuck to it.

Belinda had barely let the boys out of her sight since the drama happened. She had spent ages searching the Halloween celebrations for Fitch and Stanley with no joy, only to get a phone call from police saying that both had been found safe and well – along with Artie.

Artie had never been hugged as tightly as when his mum saw him in the hospital an hour later.

It was now three days since Halloween and the world was getting back to normal. Finally, his mum was giving him some breathing space and not fussing around him every two minutes.

Artie slumped back on his pillows, wishing he

could go out and kick a ball around.

"Fancy a visitor or two?"

Fitch's smiling face poked around his door. Above her, Jack appeared too.

Artie grinned. It was the first time he'd seen his friends since the dramatic events of Halloween.

"Come in. We've got a lot to talk about."

Fitch bounced over and plonked herself on the end of the bed. Jack, meanwhile, sat on Artie's video games chair.

His damaged arm was wrapped up in a sling but, apart from a few cuts and bruises, he had come through mainly unscathed.

Jack and Fitch explained their adventures – with regular questions from Artie.

All three had spoken to the police.

Gillian's body had never been found. Yet detectives had discovered a set of clothes covered in a strange green slime in the driver's seat of the car.

Artie nodded grimly: "I told the cops that the same thing happened to Berry.

"One of the officers told me the green goo was being tested in one of their top labs. We are still waiting for the results."

Jack scratched his nose, deep in thought: "How did you even know about their weakness for light?"

Artie shrugged: "Completely by accident, to be honest. Birch set off a powerful security lamp in one of the gardens as I was trying to escape. It hurt him pretty bad.

"So, when Berry was hunting me down, I guessed my phone's flashlight could probably hurt them as well. I tried to tell you all so you'd be able to use it against them, but there was no signal as you know."

Fitch blew her nose gently and then clicked her fingers: "So intense light burns them … and that's why they always wear glasses?"

Artie nodded: "Yes. They were hurrying to catch me so left their glasses back in the house. It cost them dearly in the end."

The three friends sat in silence for a moment.

Jack fidgeted in his seat.

"Artie, I need to ask what happened to you?"

Artie grinned. He told them at length about sneaking into the house, the garden chase, his confrontation with Berry, how the goblin melted into the ground and his discovery of the car.

"Berry had never meant to give them away but instead he had led me straight to their getaway. I knew I had to slow them down as much as possible."

Fitch chimed in: "Well, it worked! I've never seen such a mess as that car when that horrible woman was trying to escape.

"So, Eason, where did you find that huge piece of metal in the middle of the woods?"

Artie smiled: "Ah, the reflection that stopped the old girl in her tracks? The back of the advertising hoarding.

"When people put up new adverts, they often dump the old metal ones behind it.

"I picked the shiniest one I could find and dragged it in front of the car. It would be too dark out there to wear protective glasses so I knew that wouldn't be a problem.

"All we needed to do was panic her into switching on the lights rather than letting her drive away with no lights. Luckily, Fitch's awesome aim with a couple of rocks sorted that one out."

They laughed as Fitch flexed her biceps with a wide grin on her face. After all they had been through, it felt amazing to relax.

A small voice piped up: "What about the other bad guys? Did the police get them?"

The friends jumped and saw Stanley standing at the door.

His face was covered in cuts and bruises – yet he had been given the all clear from the doctors too.

Fitch wiped her nose: "Sorry buddy. No. When the police reached the house, Ridgeon was gone.

"All they found was the wire that we tied him up with. It had been hacked to pieces. Nothing else was there.

"And Birch has not been seen since Jack sent him for a swim in the tunnel. Once the water level dropped, the police combed the tunnels and found nothing.

"Apparently, there were a total of four exits along the route. All the houses involved had been rented under false names. They were not homes. That's why they looked so boring and unloved. They did not have anyone living in them.

"Still, we had a lucky escape. I guess even more children could have been targeted if your big brother hadn't stopped it."

Stanley hitched himself on to the bed between Fitch and Artie.

"The police found nothing? Are you sure? How could that be? What was in Gillian's bag?"

They stared at the younger boy.

"What bag?"

Stanley pulled a face: "You know, the brown handbag. She wouldn't let it go."

Fitch put an arm round him.

"The police didn't find anything in the car, Stan. Just a load of broken glass and her clothes that were covered in stinky green ooze.

"Are you sure about the bag?"

Stanley shrugged.

He had been so tired that evening, perhaps he had been wrong.

Embarrassed, he scooted off the bed and moved to the door.

He stopped on the way as he spotted the walkie-talkie that Artie had taken from the goblins' table the other night.

"Oooh, Artie. Can I borrow this? I can use it in my next adventure!"

Artie wafted a hand lazily. "Yes, of course. Don't break it though!"

Smiling from ear to ear, Stanley scooped up the radio and raced out of the room with his new prize.

They waited to speak until Stan's footsteps faded away.

Fitch spoke first: "Bless him. He's been through so much. I think he's a little confused.

"Mind you, I can't blame him. Who would have thought goblins have to eat children's imaginations to stay alive?"

Artie shook his head: "I know. It makes no sense. They have been living among us for years and the human race didn't even know.

"Or if the military did know, they've been keeping it very, very quiet!

"We know in future what to look for: if anyone has unexpected nosebleeds for no reason, then we could well have the answer for them!"

Fitch looked at him.

"Nosebleeds? What do you mean?"

Artie laid back on his pillow, suddenly feeling waves of tiredness wash over him. He had not spoken this much in days.

He replied: "Yeah, I overheard that from them too.

"If they do manage to steal your imagination, then you get nosebleeds as a result. It is a dead giveaway."

Jack piped up: "Well, it's a good job you rescued Stanley when you did. There's definitely nothing wrong with his imagination!"

The boys laughed. Fitch smiled and wiped her nose again.

She pushed the tissue straight back into her trouser pocket without a second thought and failed to notice the flashes of bright red that were stained upon it.

45. WARNING

Stanley had not been able to sleep properly since Halloween.

He felt tired but, whenever he closed his eyes, Gillian's wild-eyed face popped into his mind. The wicked woman haunted him even though he knew she was gone.

The house was quiet.

His mum had gone to bed ages ago and Artie had not left his room in days as he fought off his poorly chest.

Stanley knew he should have been asleep by now. And he wanted to sleep so badly.

A loud crackle broke the silence.

Stanley sat up in bed.

He looked around to see the source of the noise.

It was coming from the walkie-talkie, the one that he had borrowed from Artie earlier in the day.

He slipped out of bed and walked barefoot to the radio on his desk.

Stanley picked up the walkie-talkie and pressed the button.

"Hello?"

Nothing but static.

Stanley repeated: "Hello. Stanley here. Who's there?"

More crackles.

And then a familiar voice rang out.

"Tell your brother we are coming for him and all his friends. No-one will ever beat us – ever. We will see you all soon."

Stanley knew the voice only too well.

It was Ridgeon.

And he was not finished either.

"Surprised to hear from us, Stanley? Well, we retrieved Gillian's brown bag from the car that had the girl's imagination inside.

"It is not much to eat but it is enough to keep us both alive for another year or so.

"Then we'll be hungry again … and you know what will happen then."

Stanley dropped the radio.

It shattered into numerous pieces on the carpet and fell silent.

Stanley did not try to clear it up. He hopped back into bed and hid under the covers. The monsters were out there somewhere. And they were waiting.

NOTE FROM THE AUTHOR

Halloween is supposed to be fun. Fancy dress, buckets overflowing with sweets, families out in the streets spending time together.

The Pumpkin Code is not anti-Halloween, but it does seek to highlight the perils of stranger danger, particularly when you are old enough to go out without adult supervision.

This book took a long time to write. It is certainly a far cry from the Charlie Fry Series, which made my name as an author.

The reaction from schoolchildren though, whenever I told them about the upcoming book, has been incredible. They seemed to love the story despite only hearing the short teaser. With this level of interest, I realised it needed to be written – and this level of excitement spurred me on. I hope I have done justice to those expectations.

It was a challenge not having the four main characters in the same room together until the penultimate chapter. My favourite part is easily Fitch and Stanley's story. Fitch is – in my mind – the book's star, and a character that I love dearly. Her never-say-die attitude is reflected throughout the entire book. She plays a key role in the chapter where Stanley disappears, which brought me out in cold sweats as I typed. Even I didn't know what was going to happen at that point.

It is one of the reasons why I love writing.

I hope you enjoyed the Pumpkin Code. It is aimed at slightly older kids than my previous work, as reflected in the storyline.

What next? A good question. I had only finished the first draft of this book a fortnight earlier when my friend Eva asked me when I was writing a sequel. The answer is … no idea! Perhaps a young adult story about rats. Although I'll change my mind in the coming months, no doubt.

Thank you for reading. And always, always believe.

**

Martin Smith lives in Northamptonshire with his wife Natalie and daughter Emily.

He is a qualified journalist and spent 15 years working in the UK's regional media.

He has cystic fibrosis, diagnosed with the condition as a two-year-old, and wrote the bestselling Charlie Fry Series to raise awareness about the life-limiting condition.

ACKNOWLEDGMENTS

The Pumpkin Code has taken a lot of work.

It has been written by Martin Smith but many people have been involved in the project over the past year.

They are:

Brian Amey – the man who created the wonderful cover. He initially doubted that I could write a book about pumpkins – I am pleased to have been able to prove him wrong.

Eva Sansom and Annabel Bradshaw – these two stars volunteered to read the first draft and then provided invaluable input and advice on the plot.

Alicia Babaee – when a story begins to make my head spin, I simply pass it over to my favourite video games expert to put everything back on track. Winner, winner, chicken dinner.

Richard Wayte – the veteran sub-editor who provides the wisdom behind my work. I dread to think what shape my books would be in without his incredible grammatical know-how.

Emily Smith – my own little superstar, who drags us

trick or treating every year without fail. And yes, we do follow the Pumpkin Code.

The Smith, Fry and Minall family – family is everything, and mine is the very best.

And finally, a big thank you to you. I could not have done it without the readers. If you have a spare moment, please leave a review for the Pumpkin Code on Amazon and Goodreads, they really do make the world of difference.

ALSO BY MARTIN SMITH

The Football Boy Wonder

The Demon Football Manager

The Magic Football Book

The Football Spy

The Football Superstar

The Charlie Fry Series is available via Amazon in print and on Kindle today.

Follow Martin on:

Facebook
Facebook.com/footballboywonder

Instagram
@charliefrybooks

Made in the USA
Monee, IL
29 September 2020